HAPPILY EVER AFTER

HAPPILY EVER AFTER

MELANIE MARTINS

BOOK THREE

BLOSSOM IN WINTER V

Melanie Martins, LLC
www.melaniemartins.com

First published in the United States by Melanie Martins, LLC in 2021.

ISBSN ebook 979-8-9852380-6-8

ISBN Paperback 979-8-9852380-2-0

Printed and bound by CPI Group (UK) Ltd, Croydon, CR0 4YY

DISCLAIMER

This novel is a work of fiction written in American English and is intended for mature audiences. Names, characters, places, and incidents are either the product of the author's imagination or are used fictitiously. Any resemblance to actual persons, living or dead, is entirely coincidental. This novel contains strong and explicit language, graphic sexuality, and other sensitive content that may be disturbing for some readers.

To all of you, my dear readers.
Thank you.

CHAPTER 1

Manhattan, January 6, 2022
Petra

"This has to be, by far, the weirdest thing we've ever done."

Alex is shuffling through papers, dressed in a perfectly tailored, slate gray suit, looking like the powerful, unforgiving man that he is. Except, instead of interviewing for his hedge fund or cutting a multimillion-dollar deal, he's here with me today to interview women for *love*.

Obviously not for himself. For Emma.

Aspen had been a warm and wonderful trip and brought my husband and me closer than ever, but some dark things had happened thanks to Margaret, and somehow Emma had gotten dragged into the drama without even being anywhere near there.

Since my last phone call with my best friend ended on such a bad note, and we hadn't spoken to each other since, I didn't even bother telling her I was back in town. I imagine she must still be somewhat mad at me, but I'm hopeful soon enough this whole mess will be solved and far behind us.

Weirdly enough, Alex is the least entangled in this whole thing, and yet he is just as involved as I am to find a solution.

Looking at him, I realize how he has made an incredible change in the type of husband and man he is, which is exactly why he's here helping me today. His mother has threatened to expose Emma and Yara's affair to Elliot herself if they don't break up, and even though I'm almost positive that she is just bluffing, she'll most certainly punish *me* and release my sex tape with Alex in Aspen before doing anything to tarnish her precious daughter's reputation. After the polemic cases against him last year, we had finally gotten out of the news and weren't being harassed by the paparazzi anymore. I definitely didn't want to start it up again.

So here we are, trying to find the perfect woman for Emma to replace Yara. Emma is longing for love, even if she doesn't say so, and she will never get it from Yara. If we can find a suitable partner that will truly love her, I'm sure she'll leave Yara in the dust.

Plus, who doesn't dream about setting their friend up with an amazing date?

"It's not *that* weird," I tell Alex, pulling my pencil skirt down as I sit beside him. We'd decided to do the interviews at the art gallery. After all, the press hadn't been too interested in it since it was still closed for the holidays, so we'd assumed our romantic interviews would have a better chance of going unnoticed here.

Alex gives me a withering look, and a shiver runs through me. When he's dressed like this, he seems almost dangerous.

It's pretty hot, honestly. "I'm not even sure why I'm here. I don't think I'm the best judge for picking out a woman for *your* best friend, Petra."

"You offered to come!" I counter.

"Because if I didn't, you'd have chosen three hundred girls to interview, and we wouldn't see you for a week. You needed me to thin the herd, my indecisive wife."

"Fair enough. Still, I appreciate you." I lean a bit toward him and kiss his cheek, and I see him try to fight off a smile and fail.

We'd narrowed it down to ten women, from professional athletes to the front women of up-and-coming alternative rock bands and from fashion stylists to business owners; I was just hoping we'd find the diamond in the rough among all of them. Even though Emma doesn't know anything about our little interview, I know her standards aren't so much about looks or career, but more about attitude and how someone carries themselves. My best friend loves travelers, free thinkers, people who buck the norms of society. But they also have to be independently wealthy, because, for someone looking to climb the social ladder by sleeping around, Emma would be the perfect target. After all, she's beautiful, young, publicly single, and from old money. And I'm pretty sure Emma's been terrified of falling for someone who would only be interested in her for her coffers and not for who she really is for years now. Unfortunately, the only way to avoid this is to look for other people living similar lifestyles to Emma and me. No dating down.

There is a quiet knock at the door, and Alex sucks in a breath. "Let's get this show started," he grumbles to me before raising his voice and saying, "Come in!"

The first woman is compact and muscular, her hair cropped short and a smile that is wide and bright. Her name is Mary Anderson, and she's an Olympic hopeful in biathlon. She's more masculine than Emma usually likes, but her friendly demeanor and easy laugh make me think she may have potential… that is, until she mentions the GoFundMe page.

"What did you say you were raising money for?" Alex asks.

"Biathlon isn't a popular sport, so I have to raise my own money to get to the qualifying competitions," Mary elaborates.

Alex quietly crosses her name off the list as she departs, and I'm sad to see her go. We were so close.

The next two, a holistic healer and a semi-professional female skateboarder, are the same stories. They've achieved moderate success in the world, but they are the first in their families to rise above the middle-class line, and they're grasping at straws to make their careers work. After a brief interview, we learn that they are also not into jet-setting or partying in Mykonos or St. Tropez which might be a problem in terms of lifestyle and aspirations. If there's one thing that Emma loves it's traveling around and attending some good old parties.

My spirits lift when one of the most stunning women I've ever seen in my life walks in. Her skin is dark and smooth, and her hair coils around her face in a mixture of blond and black. Her name is Izzy. She's the lead singer of a band gaining traction on social media, and although she isn't famous enough to be considered "independently wealthy" quite yet, her cash flow from all her performances shows she's well on the way.

I lightly tap Alex's shin with my foot excitedly, but he gives me a look that says *calm down*.

Izzy greets us with a beautiful enigmatic smile before sitting in front of us and despite being the fourth we've seen today, she stands out pretty well on paper.

Alex starts asking questions about her career, her aspirations, and her hobbies.

After a few satisfying answers, I decide to take over. "And what about traveling? Have you traveled the world a bit?"

"Of course," she says with enthusiasm. "I have been to around twenty countries, but my favorite place by far is Bali."

I can't help but nod at her. *She seems perfect!*

"You seem to be a perfect match for our friend," Alex tells her, steepling his fingers and looking for all the world like he's interviewing someone to run a company and not sleep with our friend. "She loves Bali just as much. Would you have any problem going with her for a few months there?"

Izzy shrugs, the snaps on her leather jacket tinkling. "My partners might not love it, but it shouldn't be a problem."

I pause in the middle of writing something down, looking up at her. "Partners?"

She waves a hand dismissively. "My polyamorous partners. I've got three of them, but we aren't official or anything. It's just casual."

"You're currently sleeping with three different people?" I ask, trying to clarify.

She nods, unbothered. "Uh-huh. I'm still technically single, like I said over the Zoom call. It's more like friends with benefits, you know?"

I laugh nervously, scratching her name out almost frantically. "Yes! Totally get it. We'll… uh… be in touch."

One after the other, the women we interview start off great and then as we start digging deeper into their lifestyles, hobbies, backgrounds, and past relationships, we realize none of them are a good fit.

The last woman, an entrepreneur from a wealthy Brazilian family, waits until the very end of the interview to tell us she's asexual, and we bid her an exhausted farewell. After four hours, we are officially done, so I go and lock the office door before melting into one of the adjacent chairs with a groan.

"That was *horrible*."

Alex raises his eyebrows. "That's an understatement."

I rub my eyes, letting out a heavy sigh. "Why do you think that went so terribly?"

"If I had to guess," he muses, stacking the papers we had brought with us, "the real successful, wealthy women aren't enlisted in matchmaking agencies. They're out actually doing the things that Emma wants in a woman, not bragging about them in an online profile."

"You're probably right," I admit with frustration. "But how can we just expect her to organically meet someone in the next week before St. Moritz?"

"We can't, Petra," Alex tells me, standing up. I follow suit, grabbing my coat. "She's going to have to meet someone on her own. We aren't going to meet European nobility or a soccer star on the streets of Manhattan out of nowhere. It's going to take time."

Wait. Did he just say European nobility? I chew on my lip, an idea forming in my head. I shoot out a quick text and turn to my husband. "Hey, Alex, do we have plans for dinner tonight?"

Alex pauses and thinks. "No, I wasn't sure how long this would take."

I grab my phone and check the time, surprised to see it's almost 5 pm, "I think I'm going to go out. Will you and the kids be okay for a while?"

"Of course." He looks at me appraisingly. "I know you're enacting some plan you've only just come up with. I won't pry, but just be careful."

I stand on my tiptoes and kiss him. He rests his hands on my hips until I pull away. "I will. Promise."

I leave the office, my heels clicking on the marble stairs when my phone pings. I open the message…

From the one and only Catherine Dubois:

I'm free, Cafe Blossom at 6:30?

***

The last person I thought I'd invite to have dinner with me is already at the table when I arrive, her knee-length linen dress is creamy ivory and matches the tablecloths almost perfectly. She's sipping a glass of Chardonnay, and only offers me a quick glance when I join her.

"Petra," she says simply.

"Catherine," I respond, trying to force myself to not fall into the vortex of her frosty energy. "Thanks for meeting me."

"I have to admit," she says, lowering her glass of wine and looking me in the eye, "I'm curious as to why you wanted to dine together tonight."

I look at the woman across the table from me, considering my next move. I could be honest with her from the get-go, but I'm banking on the idea that now that Catherine is separated from Margaret, she will be more amiable. I think I need to come on gently, and if she's open enough, I'll ask her about my problem with Emma.

"Truly, I've been thinking about our Christmas together," I tell her candidly, my lips curving up. "I wanted to get to know you a little better since Dad seems so fond of you."

Catherine blinks a few times, before shrugging delicately with one shoulder. "Alright. What would you like to know?"

Women like Catherine love to talk about themselves, so I give her a topic and I'll see where it goes. "Dad mentioned you come from nobility. Is that true? It's so interesting if so!"

Catherine preens, taking a drink of her wine to hide her growing smile. "Why, yes, I am actually. My maiden name is 'de Rohan,'" she tells me.

I rest my chin in my hands, playing into her every word. "It sounds familiar, but I can't quite recall."

Catherine grins indulgently. "Allow me to elaborate." Before she can do so though, the waiter stops at our table and we order some food.

We share a plate of edamame and spring rolls while Catherine regales me with her stories of her family, who are actually minor French royalty, and how she ended up marrying Paul Dubois. To my surprise, she didn't hide the financial problems her family faced or bring up how Paul came at the right time in her life. When she mentioned their divorce, I thought I saw actual remorse flit over her features for a brief moment, before being replaced by her calculating look.

"Anyway," Catherine says, "that's how I met Julia, and through her, Margaret."

I raise my eyebrows, carefully setting down my glass of water, shocked at her easy confession. "I thought you two didn't know each other."

"Well, it served Margaret's purposes for us to appear as strangers. No harm intended towards you, of course."

"It served her purpose?" I repeat, unable to take the shock out of my tone.

Catherine heaves a long sigh, her lips pressed together as she looks away, pondering for a moment whether to open up or not. "Julia and Margaret introduced me to your dad," she discloses. *Holy shit!* Even though I had my suspicions, my heart halts for an instant at her revelation. "But they asked us to keep their names out of it, given the fact they are still very close to my ex-husband."

I want to argue that deception is automatically harmful to me, but I have to keep my eye on the prize, so I let it slide. "Uh, sure. No problem. So, you know Julia?"

"Very well, actually. She's one of Margaret's least problematic children, no offense to Alex."

I laugh a little despite myself. "Maybe they'll all settle down now that they're married, Alex included."

"One can only hope. That Yara though, my bets are on her as being the next problem child now that you and Alex have worked your issues out." She shakes her head with a motherly look of disappointment for what is yet to come.

I stay silent, taken aback by her comments about Yara. I didn't know that Catherine knew so much about Margaret's children, but I simply nod, having a few bites of food as I process everything she told me so far. Well, since she's a close friend to Julia, it's not hard to imagine she knows Yara and the reputation she has when it comes to preying on young women. A quick silence settles between us, until Catherine finally asks, "Petra, why did you really want me to meet you tonight?"

I give another sip of water, trying to find the best words to put on. "Honestly, I did want to get to know you better if you're going to be in my dad's life from this point on, but otherwise, I have a strange favor to ask."

She nods, sitting back in her chair. "Go ahead."

"My friend Emma is in a precarious affair that I want to help her extricate herself from. The problem is, she only dates women, which wouldn't be too difficult to work around, except she has very discerning tastes in both women and the lifestyles these women lead. I've exhausted everyone in my own social circle, but since you're French and your own circle extends into European nobility, I was wondering if you knew any successful, interesting women I could introduce my friend to."

Catherine seems to think for a moment, rapping her nails on her wineglass as she does so. "I think I may have a few women in mind, but give me a little while to think it over."

"I hope I'm not being too forward asking this of you," I tell Catherine, meeting her eye, not wanting to ruin the tentative truce between us.

She shakes her head. "No, no, this is a relatively minor thing. I actually quite like playing matchmaker. Can you send me some of these difficult must-haves your friend has when it comes to choosing a partner?"

"Absolutely," I tell her, squealing internally. Well, well, well… This might actually work after all.

CHAPTER 2

Manhattan, January 7, 2022
Petra

I kiss both twins on the top of their heads, checking the time. Lily is feeding them while also reading a book, and I have a brief moment of envying her multitasking abilities.

"I hate that I have to leave so early," I lament, brushing my fingers over their soft hair.

Lily doesn't look up at me, just continues to feed the babies bites of their rice cereal while turning pages. "You're going to get busier and busier with the art gallery and school starting back up. You'll learn to manage the time, don't worry."

"I scheduled my classes so I'd be home with them as much as possible," I tell her, grabbing my bag and coat and slipping my feet into my boots. "I'm taking a few online and the others early in the morning."

"That's good," Lily says approvingly. "Just don't stretch yourself too thin. You're paying me for a reason, remember?"

"I know, I know…" I say. And yet, it's still hard for me not to feel a pang in my heart each time I leave them for longer than a few hours. I know I've got to get used to it, but it's still a work in process. "Don't have too much fun without me!" I tell them, blowing my children a kiss before exiting into the chilly January air. I've still got a few days before school starts, but I wanted to get the gallery open first so I can avoid the stress of it sitting empty while I am concentrating on my studies. We had advertised the gallery opening for today, but unlike the reveal party for my birthday, it wasn't going to be too much of a high-key affair. I was just ready to have everyone welcomed into my gallery and share it with the world.

Alex is busy working today, so I'm alone, jittery with nerves and excitement at the possibility of having my very own gallery up and running. I hope it can fill the space the Artemis Room left and more. I know I have a lot on my plate, but it's something I've dreamed of my whole life.

My heart keeps thundering anxiously fast when Zach pulls in front of the gallery. As I exit the car, I'm surprised to see quite a few cars parked on the street outside, especially with it being so early. I head towards the entrance, nearly running up the stairs, keys jingling in hand. To my surprise, the door is already unlocked. *How come?* I pull my phone out to call Alex, hesitating to enter the unlocked building, when someone opens the door for me.

The woman standing there reminds me of a boarding school principal, her steel gray hair pulled into a severe bun on the top of her head and her thin, tall body clothed in all black. She has silver glasses perched on her bird-like face, but her expression is polite.

"Um, hi?" I say, taking a step back, utterly confused—and a bit afraid.

"Oh, good morning, Petra," she says. "I'm Tilly. Your husband hired me as the supervisor for the gallery since you won't be here all of the time. I opened up an hour ago, but later we can go over exactly how you want things done day-to-day."

I blink a few times, getting used to the idea. I guess I'd need a supervisor anyway, and while I'd have preferred to give my input, I trust Alex's judgment on who to hire. Plus, Tilly definitely looks like a woman who can get things done. "Well, that sounds great! You said you opened an hour ago?"

"Yes," Tilly affirms. "You've actually already gotten a few guests. You picked a wonderful day to open the gallery to the public."

She ushers me in, and I have to keep myself from celebrating when I see a modest amount of people milling about the gallery, including two looking directly at my own paintings. It takes a minute for Tilly's words to sink in. "Why is it a good time though? I just picked a random Friday."

Tilly adjusts her glasses, slightly surprised at my question. "Well, because there's a huge Christie's auction in town this Sunday, so there are some dealers who came especially for the occasion. Very strategic opening today."

Wow. A Christie's auction this Sunday? How come I haven't been notified about it? "I'll take your word for it," I say distractedly, walking around the space.

The walls are covered with pieces by local artists, as well as a few sculptures and ceramics placed on display. It had been tempting to display as much of my own artwork as possible since I'd been waiting so long for this opening, but another part of me knew that if I didn't offer a large enough variety, then the gallery wouldn't be as successful. After all, having different artists is exactly what would attract more visitors and potential clients.

It feels kind of surreal taking it all in, but I fall right back into the mindset of a gallery owner and decide to spend the morning chatting with different aficionados and customers, even welcoming in some of the featured artists themselves so they can chat with the public about their pieces. It's a fun and lighthearted atmosphere and it's all too easy for me to forget that this will be a whole functioning business now, not just a dream.

From the corner of my eye, I notice a man in a well-tailored tweed jacket has been hovering around the wall of the gallery with the few pieces of my own that I had chosen to display, including my new *Seasons of Life* collection, depicting different parts of nature and the life within. I try not to stare too much as he peruses my work, wanting to see his natural reaction to everything. Though it's hard to read exactly what he does or doesn't think of it all.

Finally, I see him talking to Tilly, who has her hands clasped in front of her and is nodding sagely. I excuse myself from a conversation I'm having with a young couple about a sculpture when I see Tilly wave me over.

I square my shoulders, hoping to give off a confidant air when inside I'm a ball of nerves. *Could someone really be interested in my work!?*

Tilly introduces me to the man, who happens to be an art dealer in town for the auction she was talking about earlier. He seems shocked to have me confirm that this is the first public showing of my pieces, and immediately says that he wants to purchase my entire *Seasons of Life* collection. He doesn't even blink at the price tag of ten-thousand dollars each or try to negotiate, and I'm squealing in excitement on the inside while he writes me the check and calls one of his assistants to come and help Tilly as they pick and pack the paintings up. It's an exhilarating moment for me, and I can't wait to tell my husband about it. After all, none of this would have happened without his help and belief in my dream.

I excuse myself while the art dealer, his assistant, and Tilly work out the rest of the details about the purchase. I rush up the stairs to close myself in my still relatively empty office. I know Alex is busy and I usually hold off on calling him during work hours, but I simply can't contain my excitement, so I give in and call. To my surprise, he answers on the third ring, amusement in his tone.

"Well, well, look who's calling—my favorite gallery owner." For some stupid reason, my heart gives a little flutter at the words *gallery owner*. Something I'd never have imagined to be possible just two years ago. "How's it going so far, love?"

I giggle at his teasing. "The opening is going great! I met the supervisor you hired. She seems like she knows her stuff."

"I know the gallery is your project, but trust me when I say the importance of having a quality overseer can't be understated. I thought having her there today would let you be able to enjoy yourself a little more."

I hum in agreement. "You were right on that one. It definitely took some of the stress off. But that's not all I called for."

"Oh?" he says curiously.

"Alex, I actually sold one of my paintings! Multiple paintings, actually! My *Seasons of Life* collection! A dealer bought them all!" I excitedly say in one breath.

"Really! Congratulations, wife. A successful opening day indeed then." Alex sounds genuinely pleased for me, and it gives me a glow of happiness from my fingertips to my toes.

Suddenly though, a feeling of nostalgia runs through me as I recall how Alex was the very first person to believe in me —he had not only offered me my first brushes and painting kit but had always been so supportive, even when Dad dismissed my passion as nothing more than a passing fancy. I feel like I've come full circle, with my biggest supporter now being my husband and my paintings being sold out of my very own gallery. It's the kind of success I've always wanted, and I'm thrilled to be able to pass down this beautiful building and my love of art to our twins.

"I wish you could be here," I tell him.

"I know, but this is your thing now. You'll have to learn to run it independently. Speaking of, since you liked my choice of supervisor, would you like me to line up some other employees to get you started at the gallery? I have connections for a good personal assistant, and we absolutely need our own art dealer to purchase pieces for the Gatt-Dieren fund. You can't be everywhere at once, you know."

I sit down in my office chair, spinning it around while I consider the offer. I do need a dealer, especially if I want to bring in more popular, expensive, crowd-pleasing attractions. I would also need someone to acquire the rights to and set up temporary installations by big-name artists for the gallery. At its heart, the Gatt-Dieren art fund and art gallery would be for local up and comers, but in order to draw in crowds, and therefore funds, we'd need things to tempt people to visit and donate.

I have no doubt that Alex would hire top-of-the-line, amazingly competent people to help me run the fund, and he had done a good job with the supervisor, but he was right about one thing. I had to run this independently. And while Alex may know business, I know art. I have to strike a balance in who I hire. Business-minded people with a passion for art, not the no-nonsense sharks that Alex preferred. I have a moment imagining one of Alex's tough-as-nails employees chatting with the sensitive art crowd I know and cringe.

"Actually, I think I want to do that part myself," I tell him, having made up my mind.

He makes an approving noise on the other end of the line. "That's my girl. I'm proud of you. But if you are stuck or just need a push in the right direction, just ask me. There's nothing wrong with asking for help."

I think about how I don't want to seem too dependent on him, but we are on the same team, after all. I guess I should lean on him when I need help, even if it hurts my pride a little. "Okay, I promise I will."

"Don't let me keep you from your grand opening. I'll see you at home tonight," he assures me, and we hang up.

After a quick refresh of my hair and makeup in the office bathroom, I descend the stairs back into the fray of the gathering.

***

I look at my watch, noticing we only have a few more hours to go before closing. After I go over everything that sold today, and what pieces garnered the most attention, I realize my own paintings were the ones that sold the most. Jeez! It sounds too good to be true. I can barely believe they actually bought the paintings just because they liked them. Were they just random art dealers as they claimed? Or were they sent by my husband or my dad to buy them? I didn't think about asking Alex over the phone about it. No matter what I think, I have to bring new paintings to hang where mine were. I'm honestly a little afraid of running out of time to paint myself with the running of the gallery, the twins, and my return to Columbia, but I have to have faith that once everything settles down, I'll still have time for the things I love.

The winter's sunlight shines through the high, almost cathedral-esque windows of the gallery, casting everything in a golden hue. It lifts my worried spirits immediately, and I'm more than happy to get back to socializing and networking.

The opening day is winding down when a familiar figure enters, pushing open the huge wooden entrance doors. Catherine Dubois looks immaculate, the diamond studs in her ears sparkling in the natural afternoon light as she looks around. She spots me and saunters over, heels clicking smartly on the floor as she walks.

"Good afternoon Petra," she says coolly, pushing her sunglasses up to rest on the top of her head.

I'm surprised to see her so soon after last night. I can only hope she didn't share anything with my in-laws about my little request.

"Hi Catherine," I reply before we instinctively lean over each other to exchange two cheek-kisses. Maybe a symbol of amiable peace?

"May I offer you a glass of champagne or something to drink?" I ask, showing her the refreshment table pushed against the wall at the very end of the gallery.

"Yes, please," she answers, her lips already twisting into a smile at the view of the bubbly.

There are a few high top tables pushed up against the wall near the modest refreshment table that had been set up, so we end up both perching on the tall stools. Catherine sits her clutch down in front of her and clears her throat delicately.

"So," she begins. "I have truly outdone myself, if I do say so." She reaches into her clutch and pulls out an invitation, printed on ivory card stock with delicate cursive writing and cherry blossom decal. "I think I've found the perfect woman for your friend, but I have to warn you. The woman I have in mind is so special that if you aren't sure your friend is ready to move on, you shouldn't waste this opportunity."

This does give me pause. I want to believe that, for the right person, Emma would ditch Yara for good. But what if Emma meets the perfect person, but she mentally isn't ready to move on and consequently ruins a promising new relationship? Emma is so picky about the people she spends time with that it'd be a tragedy to have someone that she could actually connect with be left in the dust for this thing Emma has with Yara.

What choice do I have though? This is my best chance to get Margaret out of my hair, stop my sex tape from being released, and keep Emma from getting her heart broken all at the same time. Despite my hesitation, I nod. I know that either way Emma will end up in some sort of turmoil, so it's better that she has someone to turn to.

"I'm sure."

Catherine slides the card over to me, and as I open it, my pulse bouncing hard in my chest from excitement, I realize it's an invitation for two for a private art auction at Christie's of New York—the most prestigious auction house in the world. I hadn't had the chance to visit Christie's before, let alone for a private auction. The invitation read:

Join us for a one-of-a-kind experience as we auction the work of world-renowned Japanese artist Shi.

Shi, also known as Shiori Takahashi, will be present and auctioning off a special piece to the highest bidder.

I dart my eyes from the invitation to Catherine and back again, barely believing what I just read. The artist known as Shi is internationally famous, heck, she's almost like a living legend in the art world. And although Tilly told me there was a private auction happening at Christie's this weekend, I had absolutely no idea that it was for Shi's work.

Her psychedelic art had taken the world by storm, especially because Shi had never revealed her face to the public. In over-the-phone interviews, she often hinted that she visited all of her exhibitions anonymously, and the mystery of who she was and what she looked like kept everyone on the edge of their seats and clamoring for her art.

From what I have seen, her artwork is stylistically striking, with bold, black outlines highlighted by colors that shouldn't have fit as well together as they did. Her most popular pieces are of humans subtly morphing into mythological creatures, done digitally so the change can happen in real time. Shi's digital pieces are heavily encrypted and can only be seen at her exhibitions. The digital paintings, when photographed, come out distorted and blurry, meaning the only way to truly see Shi's work is to come to one of her exhibitions. It's quite the feat to own one of her rare publicly sold paintings or digital pieces. Needless to say, it's an exciting event for someone in the art world like me, but for Emma?

"Take your friend," Catherine tells me. "There is someone at that event who will be perfect for her, if she has an open enough mind."

"Emma doesn't even like art," I retort immediately. "How am I supposed to convince her with so little info from your side?"

Catherine waves a finger at me, and I cross my arms. "I'm sure she'll enjoy this event. Christie's only invites the finest people. This is the perfect set up for her."

I blow out a breath, frustrated. There are sure to be dozens of people at the auction, even if it is invitation only. Finding Catherine's perfect woman could take all night. Still… it's an event I'd be thrilled to go to with or without Emma, so I'm not too annoyed at the extra time I'll have to spend on this little side project.

"Fine." I sigh. "I don't know why you have to be so mysterious though."

"The magic is ruined if you have to have the trick explained to you," Catherine tells me with a coy smile. "It took me a lot of asking around to score this invitation, so don't squander this opportunity. If Emma hits it off with this woman, like I think she will, it's a done deal."

I purse my lips, stressed yet excited about the auction/blind date for Emma. "Okay, I'm putting my trust in you, so I hope she's everything you say she is."

"Trust me, dear," Catherine says, gracefully dismounting her stool and coming over to give me the traditional French *bise*. "She is. I don't do average."

***

Once Catherine leaves the gallery, I run upstairs to my office, already ruminating on how I will persuade Emma to join me at this auction. We haven't spoken since I was in Aspen and yet I recall perfectly well her last words before she hung up the phone: "*I've always been super supportive of you. But now I need you to do the same and to stop interfering.*"

Well, it's a bit too late for that.

After closing the door behind me, I pick up my phone, take a deep breath in and out, and press her number before putting the screen against my ear. Emma is my best friend, after all. She can't be mad at me forever. The ringtone goes on, and on, and on…

Suddenly, a stern voice starts, snapping at me from the other side of the line. "What the hell do you want?"

"Hi Emma," I answer with the sweetest voice I can pull off. "We haven't spoken for so long."

"Well, there's a reason for that," she spits out. "Are you calling me again about Yara?"

"No," I say, my tone low and carrying. "I wanted to apologize and invite you to hang out on Sunday…"

I hear nothing but a loud sigh in return. "Thanks, but I've got plans." Her voice remains clipped and I can't help wondering if Yara is in town.

"Oh," I utter while thinking something through. "I, um, I've got an invitation for two to attend a private auction at Christie's on Sunday at six pm. And, um, I thought going with you would be nice."

"A private auction?" she repeats in surprise. "Of what?"

"Of art of course."

I hear nothing but an exhausted gush of air from her side. "You know I hate that shit."

"It's gonna be a one-of-a-kind experience, I swear," I tell her as I start roaming around my office in a failed attempt to tame my nervousness. "Plus its psychedelic art with deep meaning. It's something very different from the usual postmodernism you are used to seeing around. There's gonna be tons of super interesting people to meet. You're gonna love it."

"I can't," she answers dryly. "I already promised I'd attend a dinner on Sunday night. Why don't you go with your husband?"

Oh gosh! Don't tell me it's with Yara! "Please, Alex is busy, and I want to go with you not him." I'm starting to sound desperate so I pause for a beat, measuring my next set of words. "We haven't hung out since I arrived back in the States," I remind her. "Please, Emma, you're my best friend and I really want us to move on. I promise I won't bring up Yara or Margaret or anything related to either." My heartbeat is steadily rising as I wait anxiously for her answer.

A few beats of silence ensue and I even hold my breath when she finally says, "I'm gonna think about it. I'll let you know tomorrow."

Disappointment slaps me in the face without mercy. The naivety in me truly thought she'd have accepted immediately, but now that she has decided on leaving me hanging until tomorrow it fills me with needless anxiety. "Okay," I mumble. "Please, make it happen. I'm sure it's gonna be one of the best events of your life." I know I'm being insistent here but if what Catherine told me is true then I'm sure it will be.

"Alright, I have to go," she announces without the slightest excitement in her voice. "Thanks for the invite, though." And before I can add anything, Emma hangs up.

I should have expected her apathy in regard to my invitation. And yet I can't help but heave a long sigh filled with nervous apprehension for tomorrow. All I can hope for is that she makes the right decision.

CHAPTER 3

Manhattan, January 9, 2022
Petra

It turns out to be surprisingly hard to convince Emma to join me at the auction tonight. I understand that it isn't really her scene and that she might be a bit off with me because of what I did, but I didn't think she'd push back so hard about attending the auction at Christie's with me.

Eventually, though, after some more insistence, I finally manage to wear her down, and she reluctantly agrees to join me. She balked even more when I explained that she'd have to tone down the leather and spikes which made up her usual wardrobe, but she got over that too.

I'm still confused about how I'm supposed to find the woman Catherine picked out for Emma, but the closer we get to the event, the more excited I become. It isn't just about finding Emma a date, it's the chance to see some of Shi's famous artwork up close. Maybe I'll even be able to get one of my own to display at the Gatt-Dieren gallery.

After my public opening on Friday, word had gotten out that the couple that was plastered all over the news last year due to the trials had opened their own art gallery. Tilly started getting tons of calls all day on Saturday from art dealers wanting private showings and from artists who were desperate to be displayed. Rumor had gotten out that my paintings were pretty special too, and according to her, there was a decent buzz of interest from buyers wanting to own something of mine. I'm still wondering if it is just Alex's PR team behind all this new exposure. But I have refrained from asking him directly. Instead, Alex just mentioned that maybe those potential buyers were hoping something huge and dramatic would crop up again and I'd be right back in the media, and if that was the case, the worth of my artwork would skyrocket. I had dismissed the idea, determined to stay far away from any sort of scandal in the public eye. Still, if dealers snatched up some of my pieces, in hopes that their value will go up somewhere down the line, I wasn't going to complain.

I had set up the number for the gallery to forward to my cell for Saturday evening and Sunday, but that turned out to be a big mistake. My phone started ringing non-stop and fielding calls until I wanted to pull my hair out. In the midst of everything, I know I have to take Alex's advice and hire a personal assistant to take on those calls. Since I didn't have time to interview anyone, especially with school starting next week, Alex had assigned someone from his own staff to cover everything until I could hire the perfect PA.

Now it's Sunday, the day of the auction, and I can't be any more ecstatic. I sit at my vanity, watching my reflection in the lit mirror as I brush on my makeup with careful hands. The twins are in identical bouncers on the floor beside me, and every few minutes I turn to give them a bounce or brush their tiny noses with a clean makeup brush, making them giggle.

In Aspen, I had spent almost every minute, besides my sparse alone time with Alex, with the twins, and it had been heavenly. I'd have to hold those moments close to my heart for when I'm away at school, at the gallery, or on my trip to St. Moritz.

As I'm applying the final coat of mascara, Alex comes to the bedroom door, leaning on the frame as he watches me get ready. "I don't know how I feel about you looking so amazing when you're going out without me," he quips.

I smirk at him, turning off my mirror lights and standing before walking over to put my hands on his cheeks. "Don't be jealous, you know I only have eyes for you."

"Damn right," he growls before kissing me possessively. I melt into his embrace for a second; he's warm, welcoming, and tastes heavenly. I almost feel like I'd rather stay in, but the lure of exclusive artwork and bailing my best friend out of a garbage pseudo-relationship is too strong.

"Sorry, love," I tell him, pulling back and smoothing my silk dress back down. "I really have to attend this auction tonight."

One twin burbles loudly behind me, and Alex raises an eyebrow. "Just don't forget your poor sad husband and children at home while you're out cavorting with the elite."

"Oh, hush," I tell him with a playful slap to the chest.

I return to the children, kneeling down, which is not done without considerable effort in these heels, to kiss them both on their soft and squishy cheeks. "Be good for your father, okay? I don't want to hear about any nonsense from you two while I'm gone."

They both babble in response, a mixture of "ma's," "ba's," and "da's," with Jasper clapping to emphasize whatever point he's trying to get across. I give them each a final snuggle before standing back up.

I take the clip out of my hair that I had put up and out of my face to get ready, and it falls down my back in a river of curls which are gathered into a single tie at the nape of my neck. Alex is looking at me appreciatively, and I get the feeling if I don't leave shortly, my freshly dry-cleaned gray silk dress is going to end up on the floor and I'm going to end up in bed with him.

There's a polite throat-clearing from the hallway, and we both turn to see Maria, who informs us that Emma has arrived and is in the foyer. Alex insisted that Zach be the one to transport us to Christie's, and honestly, I didn't mind. He's still overly protective, but I meet him in the middle where I can, meaning that Emma is riding with me. It also helps to ensure that she doesn't take off and go home as soon as we arrive, so in truth, it's a win-win.

Where my dress has spaghetti straps and a simple neckline, fitted but not skintight, Emma's a little more risqué. It's black, of course, fitted close to her body, and although it hits the ground like mine does, the slit up the back reaches scandalously close to her backside. To top it all off, she ditched the combat boots like I'd requested, but with her black leather heels, she also sported a pair of fishnets.

Alex and I both walk out to greet her, a baby in each of our arms, and before Emma can rush over to kiss the twins, he leans over to whisper in my ear, "Your date looks nice."

I shoot him a glare and he smirks. I'm holding Jasmine, who Emma quickly plucks out of my grasp. Emma kisses her face all over, while Jasmine huffs and tries to turn away, which only makes Emma snuggle her more. My best friend's lipstick is red so dark it's almost black, and Jasmine's cheeks end up covered in lip prints.

"You're getting my baby all lipsticked up. Let's go!" I say, my tone leads with humor as I take Jasmine back and hand her to Maria.

"Have her home by midnight," Alex jokes, to which Emma scoffs.

"If you're lucky!" she replies.

After biding farewell to everyone, we bundle up against the frosty night and head to the comfortable sedan, sighing gratefully at the pre-warmed leather seats. Silk may look nice on, but it definitely doesn't keep the frigid air from getting to my skin.

Most of the buildings are still lit up by the Christmas lights that won't come down until later this month, and we sit in silence for the first part of the drive. I'm buzzing with excitement about the auction, thinking about my checkbook in my matching clutch and how it might get some good use tonight, and while I don't know what's on Emma's mind, she doesn't look thrilled.

"What's up?" I finally ask her.

"I just hope this auction is actually going to be worth it." She sighs. "I really did have other plans for today."

I lay a hand on top of hers and lower my voice. "Thank you so much for coming."

Emma gives me nothing but a small smile, before turning her face toward the window. Jeez, it nearly feels like she's going with me against her will for the sake of our friendship.

Guilt pricks at me, and I frown as I study her face—still turned away from me to gaze out the window. "What's going on?"

"Don't worry," Emma mutters.

I slide a little closer to her until our legs bump, and she looks over at me. "Is it about Yara?" I ask carefully.

Emma clenches her teeth, but exhales heavily, laying her head on my shoulder. The gesture is unexpected but quite welcomed. "Maybe," she answers. Her honesty takes me by surprise and I silently let her proceed. "She said she'd try to meet up with me here in New York before her tournament in St. Moritz, but until now, all she has done is FaceTime me."

"So the evening plan was a FaceTime call with her?" I ask, trying not to sound too shocked.

"Yeah, it's pathetic, I know…" She heaves a long sigh, thinking something through. "The only way to meet her seems to be to fly out and attend her tournament. Though I'm not yet sure if I want to go, but it looks like it might be the only way I get to see her."

I'm silent, rolling her words over in my mind. I don't want her to know that taking her to the auction is an elaborate setup to get her away from Yara, yet I need to comfort her without her finding out my actual intentions.

I lean my head on hers. "I'm sorry about that. The Van Dierens aren't an easy family, I can tell you from experience." I let out a light chuckle.

"Was it worth it though?" she asks, her voice small. "Sticking it out even when it seemed like the world was against you and Alex?"

Crap, this was *not* the message I wanted to give her. "Well, of course it was. But Alex is a trailblazer and didn't care what the world thought of us. Yara… well, she's still married to Elliot, isn't she? I don't think she'd risk it all like he did."

Emma tenses for a moment before sighing. "You don't think she'll leave Elliot for me, do you?"

I hug her close, and she accepts it. "I don't think so, Emma. They've got kids, and an image to uphold, and we both know Margaret would never allow it. Even Alex has a hard time telling his mother no, and he's the most distant and detached of all her kids."

"You're lucky to have found someone that would risk everything for you," Emma tells me, sounding sad. The atmosphere is heavy in the car, and it's not at all how I wanted her to feel for the night. I need her to be happy and receptive.

"I am." I lower my voice to a whisper, not wanting the driver to hear. "Even if he's the biggest pain in the ass sometimes."

Emma snorts before laughing. I start to giggle too when she says, "I think he was a pain in the ass to all of us."

The mood lightens, thankfully, and we talk about what to expect at the auction. I've been to some auctions in my life, but not an invitation-only at Christie's. Although I'm sure now with the Gatt-Dieren gallery being open, I'd become a regular at the famous New York auction house. I gush about how exciting it is to see the work of an artist who is so secretive, and Emma rolls her eyes.

"I did a little digging online to see why this auction was such a big deal," she announces, causing me a surprised look. "Did you know this Shi person is auctioning off a portrait of herself and that's what the fuss is all about? It's already worth millions and no one has even seen the damn thing."

"She's selling a self-portrait!?" I exclaim, barely believing it. "Oh my gosh, Emma. You don't get it. This is an *enormous* deal. She's been completely anonymous for years and has gained all her fame on her artistic talents alone. Can you *imagine* what a portrait of Shi would do for my gallery?"

Emma shrugs. "I'll take your word for it. Hey look, we're here!"

I look out the window and realize in my excitement I'd totally missed Zach pulling up to the curb to let us out. He steps out of the car to open our doors, and Emma quickly checks her reflection in her phone camera, snapping a selfie when I insert my face next to hers and grin.

"Show time!" I say before we step out onto the cold streets of New York.

Located in Rockefeller Center, the entrance is illuminated and clearly full of energy even in the darkness of an early winter evening. Emma seems to brighten even more as we walk inside together arm-in-arm. Even she and all her darkness can't resist the excitement of such an event.

I hand my invitation over at the door and we make our way into the auction house. The vibe of the place might appear calm to an outsider, but I've been around these types of people my entire life, and I can sense how thick the tension is among everyone. All the people here want to be a part of seeing Shi's face for the first time, and owning her self-portrait would be a tremendous boon to any public gallery or private collector.

We turn heads as we saunter through the modest crowd, and as I glance around, I'm not surprised to find out that we are quite young compared to a lot of the art dealers. Emma's alternative style always catches looks from the older jet-setting elite, and while I'm used to seeing eclectically dressed artists, the dress code at Christie's prevents anything too crazy.

Realizing that Emma and I are some of the more youthful guests at the auction, I think that finding Catherine's perfect woman wouldn't be as hard as I had initially thought. Surely Catherine wouldn't want to hook Emma up with someone having a midlife crisis, would she?

We snag glasses of champagne from a nearby server's tray, and I watch Emma's face closely as she looks around. I know she isn't too impressed by the art dealer crowd, so I'm going to have to keep her entertained if I want her to make it to the actual auction portion of the night.

A collection of Shi's work is hung in the gallery outside of the auction hall, ranging from her early acrylic on canvas pieces to her more recent digital pieces that helped catapult her to fame. Shi's digital paintings are displayed on proprietary screens framed to look like canvases, and if you didn't know the paintings were digital, it would be easy to be fooled into thinking they were regular paintings—especially with the slower moving digital pieces.

Shi's body of work is all about transformation, and in her fast-moving paintings, the changes are obvious. Some of Shi's paintings, though, transform so slowly that it's impossible to see it with the naked eye. You'd be looking at the electronic canvas and the portrait of a person for long minutes with no change, but if you came back an hour later, the portrait would look noticeably more feral. It's a clever, beautiful, and sometimes scary narrative about the nature of humanity.

I lead Emma over to the rows and rows of artwork, and we peruse slowly. The auction starts in forty-five minutes, but no one seems to be rushing, taking the opportunity to see this rarely displayed collection in all its glory. Soft Japanese music is being piped through the overhead speakers, and the din of everyone's voices is low and unobtrusive.

"This is boring," Emma hisses to me, but I studiously ignore her, chatting with other guests while Emma passes the time drinking champagne.

"Do you think there's something unexpected about Shi's appearance, and that's why she's never revealed herself?" an older woman standing next to me asks.

"You know, I'm not sure," I muse. "I've spent so much time studying classical artwork that I've only recently been exploring what little of Shi's catalog is public. What do you think?"

The other woman shrugs one thin shoulder. "I've heard murmurs *she* may actually be a *he*, or maybe they may have some sort of facial deformity."

"That would only make them more popular in the art world, I think," I reply.

"Very true," my conversation partner agrees.

Emma sighs heavily, so I bid the older woman farewell and move on to look at some other displays. We end up in front of two of the largest screens that are nearly six feet tall each, showing a man and a woman, the woman slowly transforming into a lamia and the man into a minotaur.

"And this is considered art? Damn… It's like a life-sized holographic trading card," Emma says dismissively, checking her dark red fingernails instead of examining the digital paintings.

My jaw drops at her comment. Leaning over her, I can't help but say, "Emma! Come on, these are two of the most impressive pieces here! You have to appreciate them at least a little bit."

Emma snags another drink from a passing server and gives the screens a second look, but eventually, she just shrugs again and takes a drink. "I don't get it, sorry. Modern art is just weird and boring to me."

I reach a finger out and tap the tips of the wings on her butterfly tattoo, which is partially revealed due to her dress's style. "What do you think this is if not art?"

"You know it's not the same," Emma continues after brushing my hand away. "Plus, my tattoos are meaningful and beautiful! These are just…" She waves her hands at the digital screens. "Being edgy just for the sake of it. They *mean* nothing."

"Oh, I don't know about that," a short woman says as she sidles up next to us, an amused note in her voice. "You don't like it, I assume?" she asks, looking up at Emma.

I can tell Emma is working up to a snarky comment, but she and I turn our heads to the woman at the same time and… Wow. I'm not into women romantically or sexually, but she is *stunning*. The first thing I notice is her striking makeup; dark blue lipstick on her full lips and almost no other artifice besides shimmery highlighter on her broad cheekbones. Her angular eyes, so richly brown they are almost black, are fixated on Emma, who seems equally as fascinated by her.

This woman is dressed in something that seems to be a cross between a military coat and a kimono, the same deep shimmering blue as her lips, with complex gold filigree and tasseled sleeves and hems. Her hair is as dark as night and pours down her back in a straight, shiny sheet that shifts with her every movement. I had the thought that if I were to touch her hair, it would be impossibly silky. Velvet, thigh-high boots with no heels are the only thing she wears on her bottom half, the tunic length of her kimono-coat acting like a dress.

At first, I thought she was going to argue with Emma about the paintings, but I realize quickly that while she's amused, her question is also sincere. I look to Emma to see what she'll say, and it takes my friend a moment to answer, seemingly surprised to be asked her genuine opinion.

"Not really," Emma finally says, regaining her usual haughty composure.

"Why, pray tell, are you at an auction for this artist, then?" the woman asks.

Emma tilts her chin towards me. "I'm just Petra's plus one. This isn't really my scene."

The woman's gaze turns to me appraisingly. "As in Petra Van Gatt, owner of Gatt-Dieren gallery?"

I make a conscious effort to conceal my astonishment and with a smile on my lips, I just nod in return.

"You've been the talk of the town after your gallery's public opening. It seems no one even knew you had purchased the old Artemis Room."

Part of me wants to shyly and awkwardly laugh and let the conversation fizzle, but I have to be a good representation of my business, even for this perfect stranger, who might end up being an art dealer or a well-renewed critique for an art magazine. "Yes. I have to say I'm surprised to see a gallery featuring smaller local artists garner so much attention."

The corner of the woman's mouth quirks up. "As much as I'd love to say everyone is interested in seeing the young, local talents, we both know that the biggest draw is you."

I blow out a breath. "Well, if people come because I own the place, and at the same time take an interest in the local talents I'm trying to promote, then I guess it's still a win in my book."

She nods sagely before turning her attention back to Emma. "Are you business partners?"

"Just friends," Emma says firmly.

The other woman nods. "So how is it that your friend is the owner of a significantly historic piece of New York's art scene, but you're not interested in art yourself?"

Emma shifts her weight to one foot, sticking her hip out and crossing her arms. "It's not that I don't like art. I just don't like art that pretends to be smarter than it really is. Like these." She nods her head in the direction of the huge digital paintings.

The woman in blue seems even more amused, the crystalline chandelier earrings she's wearing tinkling as she shakes her head. "Maybe the paintings are just too smart for you, and not the other way around."

Emma takes a second to be offended before her face takes on an interesting, calculating look. "Oh, so *you're* clever enough to understand these paintings?" Her rhetoric question hangs in the air for a second, while the other woman just smiles in return, almost in delight. "Very well. Explain them to me, then."

I dig my phone out of my clutch to check the time and cringe. There are less than ten minutes before the auction starts. "Emma..."

But she doesn't hear me. All of her attention is now on the other woman here with us, and it's then I realize the energy between them is sizzling with electricity. I'm ashamed to admit I had forgotten, in the haze of looking at all the beautiful things around me, about my plan with Catherine to get Emma hooked up with a secret someone. Out of all the people here, I do believe the specific person I was supposed to find has found us instead.

The woman in blue takes a step closer to Emma, tilting her head to the side as she considers her. She narrows her eyes, and her smirk becomes mischievous. "Very well. To me, I see layers. The two humans are looking at one another, as if they yearn to be together, but they're still kept apart. As they change, their true ferocious nature coming out, they seem to forget about one another. So maybe at their animalistic cores, they weren't suited for each other, anyway."

Emma looks again at the paintings, and a look of understanding passes through her eyes. Still, it's Emma, and she's not going to admit defeat so easily. "Bullshit. You just made that up on the spot. It doesn't make any sense."

The woman slowly looks Emma over, eyes hitching on her tattoos as she speaks. "Is there no animal in you yearning to be free?"

Emma leans even closer to the woman until their faces are inches apart. "Wouldn't you like to know?"

Oh gosh, I'm starting to feel like a third wheel when the chime signifying the start of the auction plays over the speakers. I guess I'll just have to leave Emma and the mystery woman here and hope the sparks continue to fly. Emma will find me eventually. Shooting my friend, who seems to be in a heated argument—or seduction—with her newly found acquaintance, a last glance, I tear myself away and follow the rest of the crowd to the auction hall. I hate having to go alone but if I pull Emma away now, I'd be ruining my chances of hooking her up with someone new.

Right before I enter the hall, I send Catherine a quick text: *I think we found your secret perfect woman.*

Catherine sends me back nothing but a thumbs-up emoji. Why does everything have to be so cryptic?

Resigned to attending the auction solo, I find my seat, pick up my bidding paddle, and wait quietly for the event to begin.

***

The lights are lowered in the auction hall, and the auctioneer steps up to the podium, causing a hush to fall over the room. I shift in my seat, nervously looking at the empty chair next to me where Emma should be. I really hope she isn't getting into any trouble.

The auctioneer opens the auction with a speech informing the audience what all of the lots will be today, giving Shi a quick introduction and an explanation of why her artwork is so special and coveted. Most, if not all, of the audience already knows everything he's telling us, but appearances have to be upheld.

At the end of his speech, he says, "And yes, the rumors are true. At the end of today's auction, we will be bidding on a never-before-seen self-portrait by Shi herself, and it will be the first public display of her identity."

The crowd murmurs among themselves excitedly, and I'm exhilarated right along with them. I sit with my back ramrod straight, my bidding paddle clutched tightly in my hand. Even if I didn't win the bid for the self-portrait, I'd be among the first to see the face of Shiori Takahashi, and self-portrait or no, I'm still determined to win a few pieces for the gallery.

The auctioneer calls for silence in the crowd so they can begin bidding on the first item. When the noise in the room dies down, a traditional canvas pop-art painting, one of Shi's early works, appears on the enormous screen behind the auctioneer, with the text on the bottom of the screen reading "Lot #1."

Before I can blink, the bidding begins in a chaotic flurry, bidding paddles flying up around me so fast I can barely keep up. I decide to wait out this one, and maybe the next lot too, to get a feel for the prices and how quickly everyone is going. For a brief moment, I wish Alex, or at least Emma, were with me, but I have to be self-assured. I can do this.

Lot #2 passes me by, but by the third lot, I'm ready to roll. This one is the last traditional canvas, and it seems to me like her early paintings will go for less than the digital ones. I'd like to take home at least one canvas and one digital piece, so now is my chance.

Four paddles have gone up when I decide to make my move.

"Two hundred and fifty-thousand," I call, raising my paddle, which is emblazoned with the number 32.

There are two other bids after mine, but I put the last bid in and won the artwork for three hundred thousand dollars. Adrenaline rushes through me, and I pat myself on the back internally for getting with the program and winning a piece I wanted.

I'm not terribly interested in any of the digital paintings that come up next, even though they are exquisite. I need to hold my purse strings shut for something special. Not everything of Shi's is of the intense mythological type. Some are softer and show the artist's gentler side.

I'm particularly struck by one medium-sized digital piece in a driftwood frame of a beach, ocean, and horizon all done in huge broad strokes that, on their own, wouldn't look like much, but together form the stirring landscape.

This one is going for a little more than I expected, and I'm waffling on whether to bid when Emma slides unobtrusively into the seat next to me, patting any pieces of her short black bob back into place and fluffing her bangs. I glare at her, sneaking a bid in before turning my attention back to her.

"Where have you been?!" I hiss.

"The bathroom," she says vaguely, checking her reflection in her phone camera again.

"Four hundred and thirty-thousand going once," the auctioneer calls.

"Four hundred and forty!" I yell, holding my paddle up. The man who bid before me grumbles but sits his paddle back in his lap. Good, looks like I've won this one too.

While the auctioneer counts down and announces the piece as sold, I grill Emma more.

"The bathroom for almost an hour? Were you alone?" I say under my breath, looking around to see if anyone had noticed her late entrance.

"What kind of question is that, Petra? Of course, I was alone!" Emma insists, trying to look casual as she settles in her chair, holding her own paddle in her lap and looking for all the world like she had been beside me the whole time.

"You've got some explaining to do later," I huff, and Emma rolls her eyes.

We watch more of the auction, but then Emma leans in to ask me something as quietly as she can.

"Has the portrait sold yet?"

I shake my head. "No, it's the last item. Why?"

Emma clenches and unclenches her hands on her paddle a few times, and her eyes dart around the room. She seems almost… nervous? Emma is never nervous, so it has to be something else. Is she looking for someone special? Maybe the woman she had been arguing with?

She exhales when she doesn't find whoever she is looking for, her shoulders relaxing minutely. "It's nothing. I had this weird thought and… never mind. It's nothing."

She's freaking me out a little, so I lay a hand comfortingly over hers and she actually meets my gaze. "If something's wrong we can go, Em. No harm, no foul."

"No way," she insists. "Stop worrying."

I'm not convinced, but I sit up straight again and watch the bidding intently, trying for two other digital paintings but not winning. Oh well, I had met my goal of taking home one traditional piece and one digital piece, and I find myself fantasizing about where to put them in the gallery to garner the most attention. They'll need to be in the back, so all the visitors have to pass by the other artists' work first, and maybe…

I snap out of my thoughts when another hush falls over the room, and the preloaded picture of the previous artwork on the screen changes to a live camera feed of a figure in a solid black cloak, hands clasped in front of them, and hood drawn up so the face was completely concealed in shadow. Beside the figure was an easel with what appeared to be a canvas on it, but just like the figure, a black piece of fabric completely conceals the painting, too.

"And finally," the auctioneer announces. "Our ultimate piece, titled simply: *A Portrait of Shiori*. Once the lot has been sold, the artist will also reveal herself. Let us begin.

"Should I bid? Do you think her portrait would look right at–Emma?" I try to ask my friend's opinion, but when I slide my glance over to her, she's fixated, unblinking, on the screen. I tap her on the shoulder, and she shushes me.

"Let me concentrate," she says.

She's being a total weirdo about something, but now isn't the time to talk. I hadn't made up my mind on whether I was going to fight for this portrait or not, but I might as well jump into the fray if everyone else is. Even if I don't win, people here will remember I put up a fight.

If I thought the other auctions went quickly, I was immediately proven wrong as soon as the floor opened for the last lot. Bids are going up like wildfire; people who hadn't placed a single bid so far are suddenly throwing their paddles up like their lives depended on it. Everyone would get to see Shi's face tonight, but only one of us would leave with her self-portrait to mark the occasion.

I'm not a very competitive person by nature, but oh my gosh, the atmosphere of the auction brought out what little competitiveness I had in me. Midway through the bidding I start putting in bids myself, but when the price soars well over the million-dollar mark, I falter. We have the money of course, but would it be better spent funneled into my art fund instead of this portrait? I hesitate, and by the time it's over three million, I surrender and let the others fight for it.

At six million, the bids slow between only five art dealers, yet the price keeps going up, and the tension rises at every new bid, until one of the men shouts, "ten million," hoping to close the bid once and for all. Yet only three of them resign, and before we know it, we are at eleven million. Oh my goodness, what a stark contrast with the price tag of the first paintings. When it looks like one of the men, whose face looks triumphant, will overcome the others, a single voice echoes through the hall that hadn't been heard at all in any of the bidding tonight.

Emma, as calm as can be, holds up her paddle. "Fifteen million dollars!"

WHAT!

Everyone explodes into chatter, and I even see the stalwart auctioneer's eyebrows raise at the insane bid. I look at my friend, my mouth agape. *Is she crazy or what?* I'm beyond shocked and completely speechless.

All I can manage is a thin, breathless, "Emma…!" but she doesn't even pay me any mind, just holding her paddle in the air as all the other bidders around us lose their minds, albeit quietly.

"Uh… Fifteen-million dollars going once, twice, SOLD to —" The auctioneer checks his paper briefly before looking up again. "Ms. Emma Hasenfratz."

Emma's family is wealthy and well-traveled, but she's a complete unknown in the art scene. Some of those present know her from their social circles, but the art dealers that have flown in from out of the country seem to have no idea who she is, and frantic whispers are being exchanged all around before a storm of applause starts echoing across the auction hall.

Emma lowers her arm and folds her hands in her lap, looking smug but still concentrating solely on the screen. The auctioneer calls for everyone to be quiet, and once the cacophony ceases, it's finally time to see the painting Emma has purchased and its artist at the same time.

I want to shake my best friend out of whatever stupor she is in, to demand why she would do such a thing. Emma has no use for a digital painting, especially a piece of artwork that would be in high demand all around the world. Emma didn't even like to stay in one place for long. Where would she hang it? In her private jet?

I don't get time to ask her though. I want to see who Shi is just as bad as everyone else. A low drone of music fills the auction hall, soon crescendoing into soaring pipe and string melodies, and as the song hits its splendid climax, the cloaked figure uncovers the canvas before shedding her own cloak. Both pieces of fabric flutter to the floor, and the world sees Shiori Takahashi once and for all.

"I *fucking* knew it!" Emma exclaims, causing everyone in the room to turn and look at us. On the screen, Shiori smiles widely, showing an array of perfectly straight, white teeth. Beside her, the self-portrait shifts from a photograph of Shiori into her gorgeous portrait, painted in a watercolor style, before shifting back to the photo again.

The smooth transition between digital and watercolor is absolutely mesmerizing! Of course it is; everything Shi had ever produced had been like that, but I can't concentrate on the painting. Why? Because the woman standing next to it is the same woman Emma had been arguing with in the gallery earlier this evening.

My stomach feels like it falls to the floor, and I can feel myself going pale. Oh-my-god! Did Emma really insult Shiori Takahashi's work to her face? Before buying her self-portrait!?

I whip around to Emma, and where I have blanched, her usually porcelain face is flushed red with something between delight and anticipation. I suddenly understand why she bought the portrait, and at the same time my suspicions about her strangely long bathroom trip are confirmed. Emma had been, at the very least, making out with a mysterious stranger, and something had given her the idea that the stranger was Shiori.

Shiori, still smiling, exits the frame on screen and, to my surprise, struts out from a door hidden behind one banner hung on the wall behind the auctioneer. If everyone had gasped when the picture was revealed, they were all completely beside themselves now, as Shiori walks down the aisle between the chairs directly to Emma.

Emma stands to meet Shiori, and I hear the rapid *click click click* of the media's cameras going off as Shiori reaches her and bows her head a minuscule amount.

"Congratulations on your purchase, Ms. Hasenfratz, and thank you," Shiori says, her polite yet sultry voice pitched low enough that only Emma and the people directly next to us could hear.

"My pleasure," Emma responds and holds her hand out for what I think is a handshake, until Shiori pulls Emma's perfectly manicured hand to her dark blue lips and kisses it. The cameras go wild, capturing Emma's reaction, and I have to admit it must make an excellent picture; the American socialite millionaire and the alluring, Japanese artist.

This scenario is wilder than anything I could have ever imagined, and I'm not sure whether I want to kill Catherine or kiss her in thanks.

***

After the auction finishes, everyone adjourns for a short cocktail hour. A limited amount of press had been allowed in for the auction, and they were all clamoring to speak to the newly unmasked Shiori.

Shiori Takahashi has two bodyguards with her, two hulking men nearly seven feet tall who silently stand beside her to keep the reporters at a safe distance. She does an admirable job of ignoring them or diverting the conversation when their questions become too prying or inappropriate. She had informed everyone as soon as the auction ended that she would only answer questions about her artwork and nothing about her personal life, and no matter how aggressive the reporters became with their queries, she never budged.

I say all this as an outsider because none of the guests from the auction were allowed to be too close to Shiori. Except for one person, who never left her side.

Emma.

The older woman I had spoken to earlier stands beside me as I watch the spectacle of my friend flirting with Shi. After Shiori had thanked Emma for her generous purchase, she had invited her to join her for the cocktail hour, and the pair talked quietly, heads bowed close to each other when Shiori wasn't talking to the press.

My new companion, who had introduced herself as Beverly, seemed to be just as curious about this turn of events as I was. Well, honestly, *everyone* was fascinated with the fact that the famously aloof painter had chosen Emma to join her for the night, and I'm sure everyone was dying to know what they were talking about. I couldn't wait for Emma to spill it all to me later.

"You're sure they don't know each other? Before tonight, I mean," Beverly asks me, stirring her dirty martini with an olive on a pick.

"I've known Emma all my life. She's never met Shiori before, I'm certain," I reply, happy to play into the woman's desire to gossip.

Emma is too busy to control the narrative of what's going on between her and Shi, so I take up the task of feeding all the curious onlookers innocuous bits of information. Enough to keep everyone satisfied, but nothing that would embarrass Emma later on. Everyone knew we had come in together, so I was a hot commodity for chit-chat during the cocktail hour.

Emma's past isn't necessarily checkered, but she was arrested at a secret underground party some time ago, and her public social media accounts aren't exactly spotless. She's kept herself out of the spotlight since getting with Yara, but tonight definitely changes all that.

I have to admit, they look good together, and Emma seems drawn to the painter like she has some magnetic pull. I spot Shiori dragging her pointed nails down Emma's arm, and the heated look that Emma shoots her back under her long, sooty lashes. Oh man, there is some serious chemistry there. My plan might actually work.

Yara would no doubt get wind of the whole auction affair soon enough. It's not every day that someone unknown in the art scene appears out of thin air and drops fifteen million dollars on a portrait. This was going to be a hot topic for some time, I'm sure of it. How Yara would react is the real question. She couldn't publicly have a problem with Shi and Emma hanging out because it would blow her cover. In a perfect world, Yara would get angry enough to call the whole sordid relationship off on her own, but something tells me she's going to be too stubborn for that.

When the cocktail hour ends, I see Shiori slip Emma a business card, their hands meeting for longer than was necessary during the exchange. Shi disappears as swiftly as she first showed up, and Emma watches her go, a wistful expression on her face

The media is on Emma as soon as she is alone. She presses through them without stopping, walking directly to me, and when the reporters become too aggressive, she flips them off with both hands. I laugh, because even here, where we're supposed to be on our best behavior, Emma doesn't change one bit.

"You're giving them a ton of material to work with tonight," I tell her when she finally makes it to my side.

"Fuck them," she says, glaring at the mass of cameras behind us. "Let's get out of here before they make you the focus of some dumb story too."

I message Zach to let him know to be ready for us, and that there may be some trouble from the flock of reporters on our tail. He agrees to meet us at the doors and then escorts us to the waiting car through the crowd. As we do so, Emma and I both keep our heads down, and I breathe a sigh of relief when I'm finally closed into the sedan with my friend beside me.

"Sorry about all that," Emma says, looking out the tinted windows at everyone still gathered outside.

"It's honestly fine. At least I'm not the center of attention this time."

She's quiet as we buckle in, but I can see how jittery she is. If I had to guess, I'd say she's still riding the adrenaline rush of the entire night.

"You know I have a million questions," I say, my tone dripping with amusement.

Emma leans her head back against the leather seat and sighs. "Fine, I guess I owe you *some* answers."

I turn my body to face her fully. "Why were you in the bathroom so long?"

"A lady doesn't kiss and tell," she shoots back.

"Ugh. Fine. When did you figure out that the woman you had been kissing and not telling was Shi?"

"Honestly, it didn't cross my mind until I snuck into the auction and didn't see her anywhere. She carried herself with such an air of importance I was sure she was a top art dealer or something along those lines but when she wasn't in the room bidding…" She holds her hands up helplessly. "I just had a hunch."

I take a minute to digest this information. "So you spent fifteen million dollars on a hunch?"

"What can I say? I'm a risk taker," she says nonchalantly, and I can't help but groan.

"You're impulsive. That's different."

She examines her fingernails, adjusting one of her many rings. "I just had to know who she was, okay? We had a connection. Or something."

The passing city lights illuminate her face, and I see a wrinkle between her brows. Something else is on her mind.

"At least it worked out, right? You know who she is now," I say, my tone cajoling.

Emma swallows, still twisting one ring on her finger. "You're right. It was spur of the moment. I don't regret anything that just happened, but I know there's going to be some fucking fallout from it. I can never avoid it."

I try to read between the lines and find out what she isn't saying. "You're talking about Yara, aren't you? You're afraid she's going to see all those pictures that were taken."

"There's no way she won't," Emma says, her lips pursed. "She's going to be so pissed."

"So what!" I say heatedly. "You guys aren't official, and I bet she's still sleeping with her husband! You're allowed to see other people."

"Yeah, I'm pretty sure she is," she admits, a touch of repugnance in her tone. "You know what? A part of me is rather happy she'll see them. Maybe she will feel an inkling of how I feel seeing her with Elliot, or how it feels when she goes weeks without calling me." Emma sounds sad, and it tugs at my heart. I know I set all this up to separate her and Yara, but I wish it didn't have to hurt her so badly.

I have a quick flashback of Emma kneeling in front of Yara at the masquerade, and a chill goes down my spine. "She doesn't want your love, Emma," I tell her softly. "She wants your surrender and obedience. That isn't a relationship you need, honey."

"Don't 'honey' me," Emma snaps, and I flinch, but before I turn away, she grabs my wrist. "Fuck, I didn't mean that. I'm just a mess of emotions tonight. I'm sorry."

I pat her hand, letting her outburst slide. She's hurting, and at the same time, probably excited about the prospect of something new. "Forget about Yara for right now. She's not here. What are your plans with Shiori?"

"All she said was 'we'll see each other again' and handed me her card. Actually–" She pauses, reaching into her small leather bag and pulling out the card Shiori gave her. She slides her thumb over it, causing a second identical card to slide out from behind the first. "She said this one was for you. She'll be in contact about having an installation at your gallery."

I gingerly take the card, which has the same gold filigree cherry blossom design that the invite had, the only word on the card being "Shi" and then a phone number beneath it. I'm genuinely shocked that she'd want to have a showcase at Gatt-Dieren gallery, it being so new, but the idea makes me giddy.

"You have no idea how big that would be for us!" I tell Emma, tucking the business card into my bag as carefully as I can so I don't crease it. "Even if I suspect that she's just interested in my gallery to get to my best friend."

Emma snorts. "She doesn't have to try that hard. I'm easy."

We both laugh, letting the tension from our earlier talk about Yara fade away. There's nothing to be done about Emma being photographed with Shi now. It's done and will be public knowledge by tomorrow morning at the latest. I'm sure the pictures are already firing around social media like a ricocheting bullet. Yara was going to find out, and Emma would just have to deal with the fallout.

For now, I'm glad she connected with someone that sparked her interest. The mysteriousness surrounding Shi was probably a big factor too, and Emma had to be preening considering she was the only one allowed close to the newly unmasked painter while everyone else had to be held at a distance.

It's almost 11 pm when we pull up to my condo, and I'm actually glad to be back.

"Zach will drive you home," I tell Emma before crushing her into a hug. "Thank you so much for coming," I whisper into her ear.

"Thanks for inviting me," she replies to my biggest surprise. "I had a great time."

"I'm glad you enjoyed it," I tell her. Then I bid Zach goodnight, and after getting out of the car, I watch the headlights come on and the car departing. Afterward I get inside the building, cross the lobby area, and get into the lift to take me to the highest floor.

I don't realize how exhausted I am until the front door creaks open and I step inside. The house is warm and dark, only the recessed lights in the walls on, turned to their lowest setting, offering me a tiny bit of illumination. I kick off my heels, gratefully sinking my bare feet into the carpet of the living room after I hang up my coat. Everything is silent, almost eerily so, and I have a quick pang of disappointment that Alex didn't wait up for me. I have so much to tell him. Oh well, there's always the morning.

I pad as quietly as I can to our bedroom, peaking in quickly to check on the sleeping twins. They're both fast asleep, arms stretched above their heads as they snore gently. I blow them each a kiss, shutting the door behind me.

My bedroom is dark too, and I fumble with my phone flashlight, so I don't have to turn all the lights in the room on and wake Alex, but when the bright light finally flares to life on my phone, it doesn't show me my husband sleeping beneath the covers like I expected. Instead, a figure is sitting on the edge of the bed, watching me wordlessly.

I jump back, yelping in alarm, heart racing. The figure laughs, and when my vision focuses, I realize it's Alex. He's in only a pair of black boxers with his arms crossed, and his laugh is low and gravelly.

"You scared me half to death, Alex!" I admonish him, holding my hands over my still-racing heart.

"I've been waiting on you," he says simply, motioning me over with a crook of his finger.

I comply, but I'm still not thrilled that he frightened me so badly. "You could have been waiting with the lights on," I point out.

"Where's the fun in that?" he rumbles, hands skittering up my sides over my evening dress. "You were out all night showing off for everyone else. I just wanted my fair share."

His hands reach the curve of my hips and slide behind me to cup my ass. Oh. Okay. I see where this is going now.

"What do you mean by 'fair share'?" I ask breathily.

I'm standing between his legs, and he's looking up at me, almost completely in shadow since the only light in the room is my phone flashlight sitting on the vanity where I had left it. His eyes look almost black when he nips at the sensitive skin of my breast through my dress, growling, "Everything." I suck in a breath, heat prickling my arms at the heady sensation of being so close to him. "No bra?" Alex asks, sliding the thin straps of my dress over my shoulders and rolling it down over my bare chest. With the zipper still up, the dress won't come down any farther, but he doesn't seem to mind.

Any sleepiness I had been experiencing immediately evaporates into thin air as he first palms my breasts, ravishing me with his gaze, the calluses on his fingers making me shiver as they skate over my sensitive skin. Lust comes alive deep in my belly, and I exhale shakily.

"You can at least kiss me hello first," I tell him, letting my head fall back when he does just that, only on my nipples instead of my mouth.

"Like that?" he asks, moving from one tight peak to the other.

"Close enough," I pant.

Alex's mouth is nearly burning after the frigid January air, like dipping a toe into a hot bath after a long day in the snow. I lean my weight into his waiting hands, and his fingers trace the curve of my upper rib cage while he works my nipples over with his tongue and teeth.

"Zipper," I manage to gasp, and he gets the hint, mouth never stopping while his hands pull the zipper down until my dress pools on the floor in a silvery puddle.

"All night I've been thinking about everyone watching you, and how no one can touch you but me," Alex tells me, pulling me closer still, and I whimper. "You're mine."

"Yes," I respond, fingers threading through his short hair.

The light on my phone times out, and we are cloaked once again in the pressing darkness. Everything is so quiet, besides the sounds of our breathing, that it almost seems like we're floating.

I sink wordlessly to my knees, and even in the pure black of the room, Alex knows what I need. He lifts himself up enough for me to tug his boxers to the floor, and I run my hands up the lines of his muscular legs. Of course, he isn't wearing any underwear. I smile with a flash of amusement. He must have planned all of this out.

We rarely make love in the dark, wanting to see the desperation and desire in each other's eyes, but there is something erotic about finding his throbbing manhood by touch only, following his legs to the apex of his thighs where he stands proudly, waiting for my touch. He hisses between his teeth when I cup his sack with one small hand and the base of his cock with the other, and I feel his muscles tense.

"Your hands are cold," he tells me, and I huff out a short laugh.

"You'll get over it," I assure him, spreading the droplet of precum on the tip of his member over the head and stroking him slowly. He's not wrong. His skin seems heated from within, and I instinctually want to be closer to him.

I jerk him lazily, wanting to take my time, but Alex has other ideas in mind. I feel his hand fist in my hair barely a second before he's guiding my mouth to the tip of his cock, and I stubbornly keep my lips closed, teasing him.

"Open your mouth, little Petra," he demands.

I consider ignoring him, but truthfully, I was hungry for the taste of him on my tongue. I obediently part my lips and he pushes inside impatiently, cursing under his breath when he bumps the back of my throat, bringing tears to my eyes.

I try to go at my own pace, but he isn't having it, moving my head with his hand buried in my hair exactly how he wants it. I surrender, letting him take what he needs, breathing evenly as he fills my mouth over and over. Finally, he pulls me off of him with a frustrated groan.

"Get into this fucking bed," Alex says, and I'm all too happy to comply. I'm nearly shivering without his hands on me, and I can't wait to be skin to skin. I ditch my panties, throwing them on top of my discarded dress before crawling into the bed beside my husband.

He scoots himself back against the headboard, and after a bit of fumbling in the dark, he welcomes me into his arms with a passionate kiss, holding me flush against him. I tangle our legs together as his tongue dips into my mouth, tracing the line of my bottom lip with his thumb between kisses. He's still as hard as a rock pressing against my thigh, and I'm becoming more and more impatient to have him inside of me.

"Hands on the headboard," Alex says, and although I'm reluctant to leave his embrace, I do as I'm told, gripping the headboard on my knees.

I feel his hands on my ass cheeks first, spreading them apart with his hands, before the tip of his member pushes against the folds of my pussy from behind. I'm wet and swollen for him, my breasts still tingling from the rasp of his stubbly jaw and the taste of him still on my tongue.

Alex doesn't ask permission, or if I'm ready. We're attuned to each other on such a level that he doesn't need to; he can feel my need just as clearly as I can feel his, charging the air around us like an electrical storm. He enters me slowly but without pause, gripping the globes of my bottom unforgivingly as he fills me completely. The sound coming from my throat is thin and desperate, and he gives me exactly what I need, until we are completely joined, and I feel the press of his hips against my ass.

There could be filthy talk, or sweet nothings, spoken between us, but tonight we don't need any of it. Even in the pitch black of our bedroom, we know exactly what the other needs, and our lovemaking is almost transcendent. His thumbs brush the dimples at the base of my spine while he fucks me at the perfect pace, before covering my body with his and peppering the back of my neck with love bites and kisses.

I'm already feeling that tight, achy sensation in the pit of my stomach, but when he leans so far forward, he completely changes where he is hitting me inside, the head of his cock pressing and rubbing hard against my inner walls and the sensitive bundle of nerves deep in my pussy. My arms shake and I cry out, but Alex is there, wrapping a powerful arm around my middle as he pumps into me again and again. The sensation is almost too hard, too fast, but I'm grounded by Alex's hot breath on my nape and the soft press of his lips.

"You can take it, baby," he murmurs into my ear.

"Okay," I pant. "Okay."

The feeling is so intense that I nearly push him off me; it's too much, but I'll ride it out for him. He makes a ragged noise that sounds like my name, and the sound of his voice breaking shoots through me. Without even a nanosecond of warning, I'm coming so hard that I feel like I might black out, dots swimming in my vision, even in the dark, as the pleasure rolls over me so hard the muscles in my stomach clench.

"Oh God," I whimper as Alex picks up the pace, sending me spiraling into another climax right as he spills himself inside of me in a rush.

He keeps us locked together, barely moving as he rides the wave of his own orgasm while my body clenches around him, milking every last ounce of pleasure from us both.

I can feel my fingers slipping off the headboard in my exhaustion, but Alex's arm around my center keeps me up until he gently rolls us both onto the mattress, spooning me against him without pulling out. I can feel his breath fluttering my hair, and I realize I never took it out. Oh well, I'll fix it later.

"Worth staying up for?" I ask him contentedly and he hums in agreement.

"I have to wash my face," I complain, and he grabs me tighter.

"Not yet."

I feel tiredness wanting to pull me under, and it's really tempting to fall asleep in Alex's arms in our post-lovemaking bliss, but I'm still in a full face of makeup. "Just come shower with me," I say, tugging on his hands to free myself. He doesn't budge.

"Alex, come on," I say, and I hear him exhale heavily.

"Fine, but you better make it worth my time." His tone is rough and sleepy.

I roll over, and we both make a strangled noise when he pulls out of me, still half erect. I cup his face in my hands, feeling his bristly stubble under my palms, and kiss his mouth gently. I could stay like this forever, in the warmth of his embrace in our bed, but a shower sounds pretty heavenly too.

"Don't I always?" I ask against his lips.

"Hmm," he hums. "We'll see."

CHAPTER 4

Petra

With Tilly taking care of the gallery and its opening, I decide to spend the day in my atelier and start a new collection. I'm not sure if it was Shi's artwork that inspired me, but when I woke up, I felt an imminent desire to close myself in my atelier and spend the day working on a new canvas. While my style is very different from Shi's, I realize her dedication and perseverance are what made her the reputable artist that she is today. I knew that if I wanted to be just as good, I had to have the same self-discipline. I've even chosen a different playlist, and for some reason, I chose the one playing at Christie's—a quiet and relaxing Japanese traditional music. The brush feels light on my hand as I let the inspiration guide me. The music transports me to winter, wintery trees, and a mountainous village, but I'm not interested in doing a realistic painting; my mind gravitates towards a more abstract type of landscape.

Suddenly though, the intercom pinned on the wall starts ringing, halting me from my reverie.

I pause the track, put down my brush, and go to press the button on the intercom. "Yes?"

"I'm sorry to bother you, Miss, but Emma is here," Maria informs me. "What should I do?"

"Oh, Emma is here?" I ask rhetorically. That's odd, I don't remember having anything booked with her today. "Um, can you escort her to my atelier, please?"

Maria agrees, and a few moments later, I hear knocking on the door of my atelier which I open immediately.

"Hey," I greet seeing Emma's face beaming at me. I give her a tight hug, and for some reason, I feel her getting slightly emotional. I observe her face, and she seems way more serious than usual. "What's going on?"

"I'm sorry to come over, but I, um…" She lets her words trail off, clearly in embarrassment. Her gaze goes above my shoulder as if something caught her attention. "Oh! That's nice." She points a finger toward my painting. "Can I come in?"

I step aside, inviting her in. "Of course."

As soon as Emma enters, I close the door behind me, and she stops in front of the canvas I'm currently working on. "You working on a new collection already?"

"Yep," I tell her, a proud smile settling on my lips. "This one will be made entirely of abstract landscapes in watercolor."

Emma keeps roaming around the studio, checking carefully every canvas standing against the walls.

After a few more seconds in total silence, I call her name and ask the same question again. "What's going on?"

I observe her figure standing at the end of the studio, her back to me. She's sporting a black sweater and a matching mini-skirt with her usual black boots, looking fashionable as always.

"Yara called me this morning," she announces with deep concern in her voice. She then turns, facing me. "And…well, let's say it wasn't cute to see." She heaves a long sigh, tucking a lock of hair behind her ear. "I know I told you to stay out of it, but she was so…rude." Then she starts pacing in my direction, her gaze trying to avoid mine as she thinks something through. "I felt like my whole world was crashing under me." She finally stops in front of me, and then says, "So I came here before doing something stupid."

I suck in a breath, wondering what she means by that. "She saw the pictures, huh?"

A gush of air rolls off her lips. "Yeah, she did." She pauses for a beat, her eyes drifting away for a moment while her lips remain pressed tight together. "I swear I don't know what's wrong with me. Why do I even care about that bitch? It's crazy."

I ruminate on her question for a few seconds. "Well, my guess is that she represents the forbidden fruit," I venture. "The fact she's unavailable might turn you on more than you'd like to admit."

"Everything turns me on about her," she blurts out, her tone dripping with outrage. "And she knows that. She knows that and she keeps playing games like I'm some sort of toy."

Emma heaves a long sigh, shaking her head. I feel a pang in my heart watching her being hurt like this. "I'm so sorry," I say, my voice just above a whisper. Sometimes that's all we can say to our friends.

After all, I know Emma isn't here looking for advice or guidance, she just wants someone to be here for her while she mentally digests the messy affair she put herself in. Her mind knows exactly what to do, but now that the heart is also mingled into it, she'll have to gain the courage to take herself out on her own.

"Did Shiori call you yet?" I ask, trying to pull her out of her gloomy thoughts.

"Gosh, I just met her yesterday," she answers, while she starts roaming around the studio, as if avoiding more questions. "Of course, she isn't gonna call the next day." She stops by the window, looking out at the view, before she turns and asks, "You know who called though?"

I shake my head.

"My dad," she answers, a small smile curving up her lips. "He was very concerned at me spending fifteen million for a portrait. The rest of the gossip didn't bother him though."

"I mean, it *is* quite a lot. I'd have called you too if I were him." I go to where she's standing, and once I'm beside her, I ask, "What did you tell him?"

"I said I was investing in art, and that I could actually lease that painting to galleries and museums for quite a lot, making it a good asset to own." My lips twist into a big smile filed with pride at her answer. It looks like she truly listened to me when I spoke about my fund. "At the end, he was quite understanding."

"That's true—it can be a very good source of income," I say before letting her words sink into me. "Wait—you want to lease it to galleries?" I repeat rhetorically. "If you want to lease it to me, we can certainly work something out." Emma smiles at me seeing how excited I am at the realization I can have it in my gallery. Suddenly, I recall I still didn't give her the Christmas present I bought for her in Aspen. "Oh! Wait for me here."

"Where are you going?" I hear her asking behind me as I leave the atelier, storming down the stairs to go to my bedroom. There, I go to the closet and take the gift bag with her book wrapped inside.

When I come back, I open the door only to find Emma with her iPhone in hands, smiling and chuckling as she types something in. Wow. What a contrast from a few minutes ago…

I feel tempted to ask her who she's texting, but decide not to. All I hope is that one day or another she stops wasting her time and energy with Yara. Standing before her, I extend my hand, showing her the gift bag. "I got you a little something," I tell her. "For Christmas."

Emma blinks a few times, observing with parted lips the bag I'm holding. "Really? Oh, I didn't know we were about to exchange gifts."

"Don't worry about it, I just wanted to give it to you now since you are here."

Emma finally accepts the shopping bag, opens it, and takes from there her wrapped present. "Oh, that seems to be a book, no?"

“Go ahead, open it,” I say, clapping my hands excitedly, burning with impatience to see her reaction.

She removes the wrapping paper and her eyes widen in surprise once she reads the title of the book. “Damn,” she utters, blinking a few times. Her fingers rub the embossed letters with delight and a smile settles on my lips, knowing exactly what she is thinking. “Well, those poems are quite timely.”

I let out a quick chuckle, before saying, “I remember how much you liked *The Raven* in high school, so I thought you might like this hard copy.”

She starts flipping through the pages, then observes the cover and back cover totally smitten. “I, um, I don’t know what to say.”

“Do you like it?”

“Nope…I love it,” she replies before she opens her arms and gives me a deep, tight hug. I remain in her embrace for a few more seconds, reveling in her warmth and friendship. “Thank you so much,” I hear her whispering.

"You are so welcome, Em.”

After releasing me, her features deepen, and become more concerned. “I didn’t buy you anything, to be honest. With everything going on, I totally forgot. But if you want to have Shi’s portrait in your gallery once I receive it, you can have it for a month or so free of charge.”

I suck in a breath, completely taken aback at her incredible offer. “Emma! The point is for you to get a return on your investment.”

“That’s okay,” she says, a smirk rising on the corner of her lips. “I’ve got the feeling it won’t be the last painting I’ll have from her.”

CHAPTER 5

Manhattan, January 10, 2022
Petra

Things had been a whirlwind getting ready for my first day back to class, but when the morning finally arrives, I find that I'm not nearly as anxious as I thought I would be. The twins had just woken up and were with Lily when I left, so besides a quick goodbye kiss, I didn't have any time to feel guilty about leaving them behind.

I'm going to go easy on myself this semester with the number of classes I take so I can manage my gallery, my paintings, and my homework evenly. Over the past year, my mind has been occupied by pregnancy problems, court cases, my marriage, and, on a more positive note, my gallery and art in general. My economics classes at Colombia would be a shock to my system, but I'm up for the challenge.

It's a blustery morning, tiny flakes of snow spiraling to the ground. Just enough of a dusting to make the air sparkle, but not enough for any real accumulation. It makes the streets of Manhattan slushy and gross, and I'm thankful for my knee-high Wellingtons over my fleece leggings, keeping me dry.

Alex offers to drive me to class, telling me that Zach could pick me up afterward while he's at work. I catch him looking at me when we stop at a red light, an affectionate expression on his face as he takes in my puffy coat, backpack filled with my laptop and books clutched in my arms.

"You're absolutely adorable," he tells me. "No wonder you've gotten me into so much trouble over the years."

I giggle. "You know you went looking for trouble, not the other way around."

"Agree to disagree," he says. "Are you nervous?"

I mull over my answer before responding. "Not really, no. After the year we've had, what can school possibly throw at me that would be too much to handle?"

"That's the right mindset to have," Alex says thoughtfully. "But just remember that your education is separate from the rest of your life. Don't sit in class dwelling on Jasmine and Jasper, or the gallery, or even Emma. If you're going to be successful, you need to be able to keep those parts of your life distanced from one another and not worry."

I wrinkle my nose. "Easier said than done."

"Did my business fall apart, even when my life was? No. If I can do it, so can you."

"Alright," I agree. "I'll give it my best shot."

Looking out of the window, Colombia's campus is alive with activity, groups of people making their way through the concourse and from building to building. I take a deep breath, Alex's words and the sight of so many other students making the first flutter of nerves take flight in my stomach. There are so many familiar faces I spot right at first glance that it doesn't make it any easier. Would they think differently about me now? I tug self-consciously on the Toboggan hat I'm wearing, hoping it's enough to keep my anonymity, at least for the first day. Most of the students my age aren't married, and definitely don't have a set of twins at home. I almost feel like I'm in a different part of my life now, and that I don't belong here. I try to shake the negativity off because I'll never succeed if I spend all my time worrying about what other people think of me.

I want Jasmine and Jasper to know that nothing stopped me from finishing my degree, despite all the obstacles that had stood in my way. I need to set an example for my children.

"Okay," I reassure myself. "Okay. I'm ready."

Alex kisses me goodbye in the parking lot, but I can see a tightness around the corners of his mouth when he pulls away. He's nervous too. Probably about letting me go alone, but no paparazzi would ever dare to come near the campus.

I'm about to open my mouth to ask him if he's okay when someone taps lightly on the passenger window. I jump a little before turning to see Matt and Sarah standing outside the car, holding hands. Sarah waves excitedly at me, and out of the corner of my eye, I can see Alex visibly relax. It looks like I won't be so alone after all.

"I'll see you tonight," Alex tells me. "I'm so proud of you."

Flush with happiness from his compliments, I give my husband another quick peck on the cheek before opening the car door to step out and join Matt and Sarah.

"Take good care of my woman, you two! Or else!" Alex yells to Matt and Sarah. Sarah giggles happily, assuring Alex that I'm in excellent hands. Matt does the same but looks slightly on edge, which makes me grin. Old habits die hard, I guess.

"He's just joking, Matt," I say, giving my old friend a friendly elbow jab while we watch my husband pull away.

"I know," Matt insists, and Sarah and I both laugh.

I feel more confident than ever with my friends beside me, and I fumble through my phone for my schedule so we can compare classes. We've got thirty minutes until classes start, so there is no rush. The campus looks beautiful in the sparse snow, unlike the streets, picturesque and serene. New York really does have some of the most stunning historical architecture around.

I hold my breath when we pass the first few groups of students, but besides a few polite nods, they tend to ignore us. I blow out a sigh of relief at not being recognized, and Matt immediately notices.

"You okay, P?"

"Yeah," I reply. "It's just so weird being back. Like stepping into my old life or something. I keep thinking someone is going to recognize me and ask me something uncomfortable, but so far, so good."

Matt nods understandingly. "I get it, but for as much as some people pay to go here, I doubt many of them are looking to gossip. I think you're safe."

"I hope so. It will be nice to at least have one place where I can blend into the crowd."

After a few minutes of small talk, Sarah asks, "What did you do for winter break?"

I tell them all about Aspen. Both are familiar with it, but neither had ever been during Christmas time, and Sarah's eyes light up when I describe the atmosphere of the place during the holidays. All the carolers, magical lights, decorations, and joyous aura certainly left an impression on me. They both groan in sympathy when I tell them about my mother-in-law staying in the same villa as us.

"That family is something else," Matt says with a shake of his head. "No offense to Alex, but from what I have seen, it seems like everyone but you and he are scheming twenty-four hours a day. I don't know how you put up with it."

I cringe, thinking about how I've been manipulated into going to St. Moritz with Emma by Margaret. Scheming is putting it lightly.

"Honestly, I don't care for any of them, besides Alex, of course," I confide. "He's not cut from the same cloth as they are. He just wants a quiet, happy family."

"Thank goodness for that," Matt adds. "I'd be worried about blackmail or something if I were you though."

At the world "blackmail," my steps stutter. As unnoticed and discrete as I feel here at Columbia, it could all be ruined in an instant if Margaret leaks my sex tape with Alex. Looking at Matt and Sarah, who stop to ask if I'm okay after I trip over my own feet, I'm horrified at the thought of them seeing me like that. Not that there is anything wrong with me having sex with my husband, but it would seriously damage my reputation and my ability to finish school if I had a highly publicized sex tape of any kind.

"I'm fine," I assure my friends, who look worried at how pale I must have become. "I just had an uncomfortable thought, that's all."

Matt frowns, stopping to look me dead in the eye. "Petra, you know if something is going on, you can talk to me, right? I will help you any way I can."

If only it wasn't a sex tape, I'd have told Matt already. He's good enough with computers that I could have turned to him for help, but there's no way my pride would allow me to admit to him the type of blackmail that was bothering me, let alone the fact that it was my own mother-in-law who was holding it against me. Matt is the godfather of my children; he doesn't need to see the ugly parts of my marriage to Alex, especially not when they involve Alex's conniving mother.

"I'm fine, I promise." I hold my hands up to stop either of them from coming closer. "I was just thinking about how much has changed in my life since I was here last time, and it's a little bit overwhelming."

"Don't be overwhelmed," Sarah says gently, and I'm comforted by the kindness in her eyes. "We're here for you whenever you need us."

Matt is lucky to have found such a caring soul in Sarah. I give her a quick hug, and she returns it happily. "Thanks guys."

All the thoughts of my potential humiliation out of the way, I'm more than ready to get inside. It may look as pretty as a picture out here, but it's cold enough that the tip of my nose hurts. I say as much, and we all hurry into the main hall. Sarah shares the first lecture period with me, while Matt is headed to a different class on the third floor. I look away politely as they kiss each other goodbye, thinking about how bizarre but amazing it is that the friendship between Matt and I has survived. Matt jogs up the stone stairs to his class, and Sarah turns to me, eyes bright.

"So," she begins, "can you tell me anything about the infamous art auction you went to? I've seen you in all the tabloids."

I laugh but shake my head. "Unfortunately, it's not my story to tell. It's more between my friend and Shiori Takahashi."

"They're saying *so much* about the two of them in the papers!" Sarah gushes, walking with me into the lecture hall. We find two seats near the back so we can continue to talk while the other students file in.

"Funny, since they were only around each other for a little over an hour," I comment, amused.

Sarah groans, sinking down in her seat. "I knew you probably wouldn't be able to tell me anything, but it's just so interesting. A New York trust fund darling and a Japanese anonymous artist? It sounds like something snatched right out of a romcom."

Out of a romcom? I contain a suppressed laugh at the thought of it. In my mind, I picture Emma swearing, flipping off the press, and smoking cigarettes outside of expensive charity dinners, and I smirk. "Sarah, Emma isn't exactly romcom material."

Class is getting ready to start, and we pull out our laptops and notebooks. I do everything automatically without missing a beat, and I'm glad I haven't forgotten the ebb and flow of university.

"Oh, I don't know," Sarah muses quietly. "Everyone knows that those with the darkest exteriors have the softest hearts."

I think about the sheen in Emma's eyes when she told me about hoping that Yara felt hurt when she saw the pictures of her and Shiori, just like Emma was hurt every time she had to see Yara with Elliot. It wasn't often that I saw my tough-as-nails best friend misty-eyed. I suddenly have an intense desire for her and Shiori to work out, or even her and someone else. Anyone but Yara. I just want my Emma to be happy and find the love that she so obviously craves.

"Maybe you're right," I tell Sarah. "I guess we'll just have to wait it out and see."

CHAPTER 6

Manhattan, January 21, 2022
Petra

Emma seems to have spent quite a good amount of time over the past few days with Shi. If what the media has been reporting is true, then Yara might become history sooner than I expected. Today Emma and I are having a lunch date, followed by a stopover at the condo so that she can see the twins.

While Emma is telling me all about the delivery of Shi's portrait to her estate, I can't help but smile and nod at her glowing face and energy. She truly seems to be on cloud nine, happiness radiating throughout her.

"I swear, she even came with the staff to make sure I was happy with my purchase and advised me where to hang it. I didn't have to do shit," she explains as we wait for the server to come over and give us the menu. "As they were delivering the portrait, I was even greeted with champagne and we watched the sunset while listening to some jazz music. It was absolutely magical."

"Well, looks like Shi knows how to treat you," I say, hoping she understands the underlying meaning of my comment.

But before Emma can add another word, my iPhone starts ringing, and by the ringtone it seems like it's work-related. I take the cell and after checking who's calling, I decide to answer. "Yes?"

"Hi Petra. I'm sorry for calling you around lunch time, but the two paintings just arrived at the gallery," Tilly informs. However, her voice is laced with concern and worry as if something is bothering her.

"Um, okay… is there something wrong?"

"Well…" She lets her word trail off, pondering her answer. "I think it's best you come to see for yourself."

My heart brisks up at her suggestion. "Uh oh," I spit out immediately. I look up at Emma, who gives me a nod of the head, as in "*We can go if you want.*"

"Alright, I will be there in twenty-minutes." I stand up and Emma follows suit.

"See you soon," she says before hanging up.

"What happened?" Emma asks right away.

I take a moment to process everything and gather my things. "Tilly said the two paintings arrived but apparently something's wrong."

We leave the restaurant on an empty stomach and instead of waiting for Zach, I decide to take the first taxi I can catch outside. Emma and I get inside and I instruct the driver to take us to the gallery.

My heart is thundering as I ruminate on several scenarios in my head. Why didn't she tell me over the phone what the issue was? Is it that bad? Did Christie send me the wrong paintings?

Emma notices my concern, so she lays a hand on top of mine and says, "Don't worry, everything has a solution."

I'm glad to see my strong and confident Emma back. "Thanks," I say giving her a soft pat on the arm.

Once the taxi pulls up at the curb, we leave the car and run towards the entrance of the gallery as fast as we can to see what the problem is.

Well, it isn't so much a problem as it is a surprise. Reaching where Tilly is standing, I notice the two pieces I had purchased are there, packaged carefully and already unloaded… As are six others.

"This must be a mistake," I conclude as I watch the eight packages laying on the floor on the west wing of the gallery. "I only won two paintings."

"Well, on the papers it clearly states our delivery address," Tilly answers, checking once more the details on the packing slip, before handing them to me, along with a closed envelope. "And here's a note that came with the delivery."

I first read the packing slip that displays eight pieces, and, after opening the envelope, I find inside a personalized card in looping, elegant cursive.

Petra,

I'd hate for your beautiful new gallery to have an incomplete exhibit, so I've included a few other pieces as a show of good will. In the future, maybe we can help each other out. After all, women in the art world should always support other women.

Tell Emma I said hello.

- Shiori

"Huh," I say out loud after reading the note a few times. "Does this seem like something that can turn out badly for me in the future?" I ask Emma, handing her the note. I have no idea what favor I could do for Shiori, and I don't want to get myself into a nasty spot.

Emma reads the note, her face thoughtful, but eventually hands it back to me with a shrug. "The worst thing I can think of is her asking you to display a controversial exhibit in your gallery, or something along those lines."

I haven't even seen the six other pieces she had shipped me, but my palms are already itching to open them and see what kind of treasure lay within. I don't think I can resist the siren song of the paintings, even if it meant I'd owe Shi later on.

"Fine," I say quickly. "Let's open them and see what we have."

Emma and Tilly give me a hand and in no time we manage to take all the paintings out of their boxes and we lay them against the wall to have a full view of the collection she sent. Three of the new paintings seem to be from the same collection as the digital one I bought; they are all landscapes with slow movements and transformations. While the other three seem to be from the same collection of the traditional acrylic painting I bought. I'm both moved and speechless as I observe the set of paintings she offered me. With four paintings from each collection, I can have a proper exhibit set up in representation of the one and only Shiori Takahashi.

"Well, those are pretty dope," Emma praises. "I like them better."

I stand before the pieces, pondering the best place to hang them. The wall against where they are standing seems large enough to accommodate the eight pieces, but I don't think the white background is good enough. After originally acquiring my two Shi pieces, I bought several shades of beige paint for the wall which were intended for the painters who were about to come on Sunday. Well, since Emma is here maybe we can do it together today.

"Tilly?"

"Yes, Petra?"

"You can take the rest of the day off since the gallery will be closed," I announce. "I have to set up the exhibit and it'll take some time."

"You want me to help?" Emma asks immediately, her excitement palpable.

A smile curves the corners of my lips at her question. "Yes, please, I need to paint the wall a different color for her exhibit. Can you give me a hand?" In my opinion, Shi's art needed more than the neutral-colored walls that I preferred when displaying other artists. With more subtle pieces, I didn't want the walls themselves to detract from the artwork. Shiori's art, on the other hand, demands attention so powerfully that they almost seem out of place on a white wall.

"Uh, alright, but you promised we'd eat and then spend the afternoon with the twins," Emma reminds me. "So far, I'm on an empty stomach condemned to spend the whole afternoon here."

"I can fix that," I tell her as I come up with a plan. I grab my phone and order Chinese food from the restaurant where we were about to eat which will be delivered in forty-five minutes. Then I call Lilly so that she can pass over and drop the kids off while she takes her break. "Problem solved. Food and the twins will be here in no time."

Once this is done, Emma and I go upstairs to my office where we leave our coats, jewelry, and shoes. She then takes her sweater off, revealing a plain white t-shirt underneath. I give her one of the smocks that were intended for the painters, and we then grab all the tools needed including trays, paints, and rollers before going back downstairs.

"How come you had all this stuff in your office?" she asks.

"I wanted the painters to come over and paint the wall to have it ready for her pieces," I explain as we go down the stairs. "But since her artwork came sooner I thought we could do it ourselves."

"Don't you think we should let the professionals handle this?" she asks with concern. "I have never painted a wall in my life."

"Don't worry, these are emulsion paints, they are super easy to spread. We'll put plastic and cardboard on the floor to protect it. I know how to do it." While I have never painted a wall in my life either, I have painted enough on a canvas, and I suppose the techniques aren't that different.

"Only you make me do those things," she says, shaking her head.

I smile and give her a light pat on the shoulder. "It'll be fun."

We first start completely rearranging some of the other painting series in the west portion of the gallery. Then we chose our favorite shade among the few paints I have and we start filling the floor with protective plastic and a few pieces of cardboard. While I'm not gonna be painting on a canvas, the fact I'm getting some manual work done on my gallery along with my best friend fills my heart with pride and delight. I take the first roller, dip it in the paint tray, and show her how to spread the paint from the top of the wall to the bottom. The concern in her facial expression deepens and it makes me laugh. "It just seems hard the first time, then it's gonna be automatic, you'll see."

My Emma has never been into manual work, but seeing her doing her best as she takes the roller and starts spreading the paint on the wall brings me immense joy.

***

"I've got uh… let's see… two fried tofu lo mein?"

I quickly take off my gloves and sign the receipt, thanking the bicycle delivery boy and taking the steaming brown paper bag from his hands.

"This is my first delivery to an art gallery," the delivery boy says with a chuckle. "I passed it twice thinking I was in the wrong place."

"Sorry!" I chirp. "I'll clarify next time."

I lock the enormous gallery doors again after he leaves, taking my bounty of Chinese delivery food to the west wing of the gallery where Emma and the twins are waiting.

Lilly had come over and dropped the twins at the gallery before going out for her break. They seem perfectly content to watch us paint while they sit in their jumpers, occasionally screeching just to hear their own echoes in the empty gallery and cackling in response.

Emma and I take off our painting smocks, electing to sit on the cardboard that lies on the floor with the babies rather than tracking down chairs. I groan when I sit, pushing on my lower back with my hands until it cracks.

"I think I'm getting old," I complain.

"Surely it couldn't be because you birthed twins like eight months ago," Emma ripostes, cracking her pair of chopsticks in half and digging into her food.

"Probably a bit of both," I agree, fishing my oyster pail of tofu lo mein from the paper bag along with a copious amount of soy sauce packets.

Jasmine and Jasper become eager at the sight of food, so I pour some yogurt melts out onto the tray of their saucers so they can eat with us. "You're still a little small for Chinese takeout," I tell them.

Emma looks at the paintings from Shiori lined up against the adjacent wall. "I still can't believe she sent all of those."

"I know, right?" I respond. "I'm telling you, she's trying to get to you through me!"

Emma is suspiciously silent, looking anywhere but at me while she chews a mouthful of rice. "What are you hiding?" I demand.

She swallows. "Stop being so fucking nosy."

I sit my chopsticks on top of my food box and cross my arms. "Don't say the F-word in front of the babies! And I'm not being nosy, actually. She delivered the paintings to *my* gallery, so I'd say it's my business too."

Emma sets her own chopsticks down and leans backward on her hands, face to the vaulted ceiling. "Fine. We've been… hanging out," she finally admits. A pity I had to learn it from the media first. "So I doubt she's trying to get to me through you. She already has gotten to me."

I gasp, covering my mouth. "Emma, are you *blushing*?"

"No! Yes. Maybe. Fu–" she slides a glance at Jasmine, who is watching her with enormous round eyes. "Frick. She's under my skin Petra, and we haven't even… *kissed*." She does finger quotes as she says the last word. "I mean, since the auction that is."

"Woah," I say, at a loss for words. "Why didn't you tell me?"

Emma shrugs self-consciously. "I saw you were in the tabloids after the auction. Not as much as Shi and I, but you're recognizable too. I know you want to avoid being in the public eye, so I wanted to leave you out of it."

I motion towards the paintings against the wall. "I think I'm in it either way."

Emma sits up straight again, picking up her food but poking at it more than eating. "Petra?" she asks.

I'd just resumed my lunch, but I slurp up the noodle hanging from my mouth to answer her. "Yeah?"

"I know it's complicated with Yara being your sister-in-law. Shiori and I aren't doing anything but hanging out, but I don't want to make things more complicated for you regarding Alex's family."

Oh, poor Emma. As hard of a front as she puts up against the world, she cares deeply for the few people she lets close to her. "Your happiness will always come before Yara's, or anyone else's, opinion of me, Em. Do what makes you happy."

Her smile is full of relief. "Thanks, Petra, I–" She stops when her phone rings, and the relief is quickly wiped from her face when she sees the screen. "It's Yara," she says tightly.

"Put it on speaker," I instruct, before giving a pacifier to each of the twins so they can keep quiet. "But don't tell her I'm here."

Emma hesitates, but when she sees the twins behaving so well, she nods, answering the phone on the speaker setting. "Hello?"

"Emma." Yara's haughty voice comes through the phone, her usual attitude not dulled at all by the slight buzz of the speaker. "I've seen yet another interesting photo and story online today. I see you continue to think nothing of me or my feelings."

Emma closes her eyes before responding. "I don't know what you're talking about."

"Oh, I don't know, maybe the picture on the front page of the latest gossip rag of what looks like you and that fine lady boarding a yacht for a private trip up and down the coast?" Her tone is sarcastic and borderline offensive. "Added on to the pictures of you sniffing up her skirt at her latest auction, can you see why I'd assume you'd completely disregarded me and what we have together?"

Yara's words should sound hurt, but instead, she merely sounds annoyed. As if she's angrier that Emma would dare to have some fun with another woman without her permission, not that the woman that she was currently sleeping with and leading on might be cutting things off.

"We're just friends. She's interesting. Different." Emma takes a deep breath. "Can't I have female friends without you getting upset with me?"

"Do you want to see me play at the tournament or not, Emma? I was hoping you'd be able to join me, but if you're too busy playing house with Shiori–"

"No!" Emma insists. "I want to come. I miss you."

Yara sniffs disdainfully on the other line before barking a sarcastic laugh. "Excuse me if I don't quite believe that. Have you forgotten all I've done for you?"

"No," Emma says again, quieter this time.

"Good." Yara's tone is clipped. She's decided the conversation is over. "Expect your invitation in your inbox soon. Don't keep me waiting. You're on thin ice with me."

Yara hangs up without another word, and Emma looks thunderstruck as she stares at the silent phone in her hand. I can't believe what I just heard; how Yara completely tore down the usually defiant Emma with just a few ugly phrases. I've never been more upset at Alex's sister as I am now watching my friend rub her eyes with her hands, covering up what I assume are tears in the corners of her perfectly lined eyes.

"What a frigid bitch," I say through clenched teeth before I could stop myself. I notice both babies looking at me, and Jasper forming the "b" sound over and over with his lips. "Shoot, pretend you didn't hear that!" I amend, pressing one of the musical buttons on each of their Exersaucers.

I turn back to my friend, both of us still sitting on the cardboard on the floor of the gallery. "Don't go to St. Moritz, Em. Don't put yourself through that."

She looks down at the ground. "I have to. I've been waiting for weeks now to see her. I already promised I'd be there."

"But what about Shiori–" I start, and Emma cuts her hand through the air, signaling for me to stop.

"Shiori is just a friend," Emma says sternly, as if she's trying to convince both herself and me. "Yara is…*more*. I have to go and see her."

Like hell you do! I want to yell, but nothing is going to change her mind. Even if she told Yara she wasn't coming, that wouldn't be the end of it. Yara would stomp her feet, complain, and guilt trip Emma into coming, no matter what. For the first time, I'm glad that I'm stuck accompanying her. She's going to need some backup, and maybe my presence will help keep Yara on her best behavior.

"Okay," I acquiesce, giving Emma an understanding smile. "I won't argue with you about relationship stuff. You're a big girl."

Emma smiles reluctantly. "Yeah, I'm a big girl." She laughs, holding up a yogurt melt for Jasmine. "And us big girls have to stick together, right, Jas?"

Jasmine coos, taking the yogurt melt in a slobbery hand and eating it.

I go to put the rest of my food back in the bag for later, but my eyes land on the eight pieces from Shiori, and an idea forms in my mind. We all needed to stick together, right? Maybe that includes Shiori too.

"Emma, watch the babies for a minute. I've got to make a phone call."

I don't trust the echoes of the gallery to not tip Emma off to my plan, so I head out to the front steps of the building and pull out my phone, finding the newest contact I had entered just a few days ago.

Shiori picks up right away, her voice calm and melodic. "Petra."

"Shiori," I reply. "First off, thank you so much for the paintings."

"Oh, you're most welcome," she says, her tone warm. What a big contrast with Yara's! "As I said in the letter, we women have to look out for each other."

"You're right, and that note made me think quite a bit. Um, well, I have to ask you something a little more personal." I pause for a breath, mentally getting ready to go forward. "What are your intentions with Emma?"

Shiori is silent before her tinkling laughter comes over the line. "Are you her keeper? Why must I tell you?"

I kick myself mentally. I should've been less blunt. "No… I mean… do you like her?" I close my eyes, feeling even more foolish. "I don't know how to say this without either sounding crass or like I'm in elementary school. Are you interested in her romantically?"

Shiori sounds amused when she speaks next. "The path Emma and I are currently walking together is one I would like to continue on. Does that help?"

Sort of? "Yes, it does," I say instead. "So I want to suggest something to you."

I might be messing up royally here, but I give Shi a quick rundown of everything happening between Yara and Emma. To her credit, Shi seems genuinely angry when I explain how emotionally manipulative my sister-in-law can be, which leads me to believe she really has feelings for Emma. I finish up telling Shi about St. Moritz and inviting her to come. It would be the last place the public would expect a famous artist to show up out of nowhere, but she'd absolutely be welcomed at the festivities at the tournament.

"I've never been to Switzerland," Shiori muses. "Is it beautiful?"

"Very," I assure her. "They play on a frozen lake in a mountainous valley. It's breathtaking."

She's quiet for a moment, and when she speaks again, she sounds almost vulnerable. "And you're sure Emma won't be angry at me for interfering?"

"Just have your manager call the tournament officials and they'll be falling all over themselves to have you come. She never needs to know we orchestrated this."

Shiori sighs. "I will think about it. Going seems like a very large step in a very new relationship, especially if there is someone else competing for her heart. Give me some time to consider this."

"Thank you, Shiori," I tell her, and we conclude the call.

This could go very well, or very badly. Either way, I was in the thick of it now whether or not I wanted to be.

CHAPTER 7

Manhattan, January 27, 2022
Petra

Moonlight pours in through the frosted windows of the nursery, the only illumination in the room. I stand in Alex's arms, my back to his front, as I finish saying goodbye to the twins. It's 9:30 pm, and the company's plane is waiting at Teterboro for me, but I can't seem to tear myself away from this silvery, silent room and my husband's embrace.

"Do you want me to join?" Alex whispers.

"No, don't worry," I tell him, my eyes still pinned on my sleeping babies. "It's just gonna feel so odd being away from them for so long." Suddenly, my worst fear settles in my mind and I can't help but share it out loud. "What if something happens and I'm not here for them?"

"Everything will be alright," Alex rumbles in my ear, followed by a press of his lips to my hair. "You're going to put this nonsense with my mother, my sister, and your friend to rest and come back home. It's only four days."

Alex still believes that I have to go because if I don't succeed in tearing Emma away from Yara, his mom will ruin my friendship with my bestie forever.

In reality, I know Margaret has my sex tape with Alex and will reveal it if I fail. Either way, I'm screwed. This is why I'm standing here, my luggage already in the car's trunk, which is idling outside of the condo.

"I don't want to be across the world from you. From them." I turn to bury my face in his shoulder, and he lets me, stroking my back.

"Just think of it like this. When you wake up, it will be Friday and you'll be home by Monday. It's just the weekend. That isn't long at all. You can do this. I promise nothing will happen to the twins while you are away."

I know he's right. More so, I know I don't have any choice in the matter. Somehow everything has ended up on my shoulders, and I have only this short time to fix it. Except, I can't seem to physically make my feet move from this nursery away from the twins.

"Send me pictures and videos, okay?"

"Of me having fun with them without you? You bet I will," Alex tries to tease me, but it just falls flat. Realizing I'm not cheering up, his face deepens and he clears his throat. "Alright, I promise."

I can hear Jasmine and Jasper's slow, sleeping breaths, and I close my eyes to soak in the sounds and smells of them. It makes a knot form in my throat again, and I press my hand against it, willing myself not to cry.

"Fuck Margaret," I whimper. "I hate her."

Alex flinches but doesn't scold me. He just holds me, rocking us back and forth, so warm and solid. I think about us being catapulted into the tabloids again for a raunchy sex tape leaked online, and how it would strain the tenuous happiness he and I had finally found together. Everything, besides Margaret's scheming, was peaceful now. I wanted it to stay this way.

But jeez, I really really hate all the dramas I'm about to dive into headlong.

Emma knows something's up with me going with her to Switzerland, but I think she's relieved enough to have someone with her that she won't ask too many questions. She knows Margaret has some sort of power over me, but she isn't sure what. To her, the important thing is she doesn't have to face Yara and their spiraling affair alone.

The one bright spot in all of this is that I have a secret weapon up my sleeve, if all goes correctly that is. No one but me knows that Shiori Takahashi has snagged a VIP invite to the St. Moritz Snow Polo World Cup celebrations, and if Shiori decides to attend, I'll have the dual pleasure of making Emma happy and pissing Yara off, all at the same time.

Shiori and Emma just make sense. Emma is a traveler and adventurer and Shiori, an artist ready to scour the world for inspiration, from the smallest village to the highest peaks. They are a perfect pair. All that stands in their way is Yara.

"Fuck Yara too," I say into Alex's shoulder, and he sighs heavily.

"Do you like *anyone* I'm related to?" he asks me softly, his voice both sad and amused.

"Only you and the twins," I assure him. "Everyone else can get f–"

Alex puts a finger over my lips. "That's enough. You've been hanging out with Emma too much."

I huff a laugh and his arms tighten around me. We stay like that for more long minutes in the cold winter starlight before he lets his arms fall away, tilting my chin up so I look into his cerulean eyes. "It's time to go, little Petra."

I try to look over at the cribs once more, but Alex pinches my chin gently between his thumb and forefinger, keeping my eyes on him. "You've already said goodbye a hundred times. They're sleeping and doing it another time is just going to cause you more pain. Let's go."

Sniffling, I nod and let him lead me out of the nursery. Even though every motherly instinct is telling me otherwise, I don't look back. Alex is here. Lily is here. Even my dad is nearby. My babies are not alone, no matter how lonely I seem to feel without them.

***

It's pitch black out when I kiss Alex goodbye and climb into the black sedan, feeling heartsick. There's nothing to be done about it now, though. I'm on my way to Switzerland, and I might as well get over it.

To distract myself from how badly I want to turn around and go home, I go over my plans for the next three days. Once we land in Switzerland at around 10 am, our driver will take us to Badrutt's Palace for check-in, and we'll then head to our rooms for a quick refresh, before going to see Yara's match.

According to what I found out about the Snow Polo Tournament, she's captain of Team Badrutt's Palace, and the media is in a frenzy to see her and her team, composed of all men aside from herself. Yara has a private residence a short way up into the mountains, and she is convinced that Emma will be staying with her. I had insisted that we rent a separate room just in case Emma wants to get away from Yara for a night, or even a few hours, but unless Shiori shows up, I'm afraid Emma might actually take Yara up on her invitation.

Once the sun begins to set, it'll be too cold to play, and the parties and celebrations will begin. The snow polo teams are small, but the number of people who are coming to watch outnumbers them by the hundreds. There are only two games a day, which leaves plenty of time for socializing. With St. Moritz being difficult to get to, expensive, and tickets to the matches being sparse, only the wealthiest and most elite sports fans would be attending.

I am not a sports fan by any stretch of the imagination, but I get the feeling there will be a lot of attendees like me. Mostly present for the parties and networking, less for the polo. Being able to be at the St. Moritz Snow Polo World Tournament is, from what I read online, a status symbol in and of itself, and no sports knowledge is necessary.

Judging from the string of annoyed texts on my phone, Emma has already boarded the jet and is waiting less than patiently for me. She had her own family jet, but Samedan Airport could only handle a certain number of flights a day, and with Emma and I being last minute additions to the event, it made more sense for us to fly together instead of arriving at different times, or even worse, landing at the public airport and having to drive for over five hours to reach St. Moritz alone.

I yawn hugely, seeing the lights of Teterboro out the window. The only awkward part about flying in with Emma would be sharing the bed in the plane's bedroom, but it's a king-size mattress anyway. Plus, Emma and I had slept on worse in our younger days. The thought makes me smile to myself. How weird is it that just a few years ago I would be ecstatic to be boarding a plane and traveling to an exclusive event in the Swiss Alps with my best friend, not a single worry in the world? Now, I'm leaving not just a husband behind, but my children and my business. I could never have imagined feeling this way.

My driver unloads my luggage while I grab my carry-on bag, stifling another yawn as I trot reluctantly towards the plane, which is already lit up with the stairs let down for me. This airport isn't very busy at this hour, and besides the whooshing of my plane's engine, it's a beautiful evening.

Emma, dressed in a black romper and without a stitch of makeup, is reclining in one of the beige leather seats, a cup of something steaming clutched in her hands. Her dark, blood-red nails tap a *click click click* cadence on the ceramic cup, her eyes narrowed and following me as I board.

"Look who finally decided to join us," she says sarcastically.

"Oh, shut up," I respond, my nerves raw from having to take this unnecessary trip. "Why are you drinking coffee when we're going to sleep through this entire flight?"

"It's hot chocolate with Baileys," she informs me, before taking a sip.

I raise my eyebrows appraisingly. "Is it vegan?"

"Yep," she responds. "This is made with almond milk." She takes another drink, observing me attentively. "Are you okay?"

"Sorry," I mutter, falling into the seat across from her. "It's just hard to pull away. From the babies and Alex, I mean."

Emma pages the flight attendant, who soon brings me a large round mug just like Emma's full of hot chocolate and Baileys Irish Cream. I take a long sip and sigh, eyes fluttering. Delicious.

"I figured that's why you were late," Emma says, sounding sadder than I expected. I look up at her and she's looking out the window wistfully. "I know you've got a lot here, but I can't say that I'm not looking forward to traveling with you. It's been a long time since we've escaped like this."

"I was thinking the exact same thing on the ride over," I admit. "I think once the sadness subsides from having to leave the twins, I'll be a lot more excited. We always have fun, don't we?"

Emma smiles a little, looking from the window over at me. "Yeah, we do. Even if we're going to see my vengeful lover play polo."

"It's a first, that's for sure," I say with a giggle.

Takeoff is uneventful, and before I know it I'm draining my mug of hot chocolate and we're in the air, leaving New York and my family far behind. Switzerland is an incredibly long flight away, but my company is good, and the plane's bedroom is at least familiar. I have to remind myself I came here with a clear mission: making sure Emma and Yara's affair ends once and for all.

Looking at Emma who seems more pensive and worried than usual, I say, "Is everything alright, Em?"

She heaves a long sigh, her eyes never leaving the window. "I'm fine, I'm fine…" And yet, her tone seems to indicate otherwise. "Just excited to see her," she announces.

I keep quiet for a moment, ruminating on a few questions I have in mind that would help Emma see with clarity how Yara is treating her. "Can I ask you something?"

"Sure," she answers, her eyes finally meeting mine.

I ponder for an instant the best words to formulate my question. "Doesn't it bother you sharing the same person with someone else?"

She blinks a few times, clearly confused. "How so?"

"Well, you and Elliot are basically sleeping with the same woman. Doesn't it bother you?"

"It's not really like that," she retorts, shifting in her seat. I raise an eyebrow at her words, waiting for her to dwell further. "Yara said her marriage sex life was dead and she and Elliot hardly ever sleep in the same bed let alone for pleasure."

What? My jaw drops at her revelation. That doesn't make sense! Yara literally has his initials marked on her skin. Why on earth would they sleep in separate bedrooms? "How come?" I ask immediately, trying to digest the news. "Did she tell you why?"

"No, she didn't. But sexless marriages aren't unusual."

I frown at her answer, unable to believe it. Does Elliot already know something about the affair? Or is Yara just bluffing to reassure Emma? As I come to think of it, that might explain why Margaret has been so worried about the affair. Maybe she has seen Yara and Elliot's relationship deteriorate over the past few months because of Emma. I'm momentarily taken aback as I realize Emma had never told me about it before. It's hard to believe Elliot and Yara are in a sexless marriage, though. But either way, I'll soon find out the truth.

Looking out of my window to the clouds surrounding us, I try to convince myself that this will be a fun adventure and a much-needed break from the twins. After all, I haven't traveled with my best friend since I got married, and from what I saw online, the hotel looks absolutely fantastic with its views of the frozen lake and mountains. Plus, this will be good practice for me to network with wealthy investors for my art fund and get my name out there.

The only dark spot on the horizon is Yara, but the cracks in her pseudo-relationship with Emma are already starting to show, and if I'm lucky, this weekend will turn those cracks into trenches. Then, once I return home, I can put Margaret and her nonsense out of my mind again for a long while.

I look at Emma's sleepy profile as she finishes her drink and tries hard not to doze off in her seat. If I'm *really* lucky, I'll get everything plus a happy ending for my best friend and godmother to my children. I got my once-in-a-lifetime love, so now it's her turn.

CHAPTER 8

St. Moritz, January 28, 2022
Petra

"I'm beginning to think it's going to be winter forever," I tell Emma, pulling on my gloves as the plane comes to a stop on the tarmac at Samedan. When I look out the window, all I can see is white, white, and more white.

The landing had gone off without a hitch, even if it had looked terrifying as the plane circled down into the mountain valley and onto the short runway. Emma and I had crawled out of bed about an hour beforehand and were having our coffee and breakfast before the nerve-wracking landing. Now it's time to disembark and head to the hotel. I give a quick double check to make sure I've not left anything behind. Once that's done, I'm more than eager to check my phone. I power it on, immediately texting Alex that I've arrived safely. He responds in seconds, which makes me grin, knowing that he had been waiting for my message.

What I don't expect is the message that pops up right afterward… from Yara.

Don't say anything to Emma, but you and I need to talk. I'm sending a separate car for you. Make an excuse.

My stomach flutters. Are we getting into all this already? I haven't even gotten off the plane yet!

I'm going to the hotel first, I reply.

She's as quick to text back as her brother. *Absolutely not. We're going to settle this now. I'll see you in 20 minutes.*

I feel like throwing the phone across the plane, but I take some deep breaths to center myself, trying to think up a way to explain to Emma why I have to leave immediately before we even get to our rooms. It's impossible, and as much as I don't want to piss off Yara even more before our talk, she's just going to have to get over it.

No. I'll come to your villa after we check in. There's no other option, I type.

The bubble pops up, showing that she's typing, but she stops multiple times, before sending me a brief message.

Fine. I'm unavailable in 2 hours, arrive before then.

It'd be cutting it close, but it'd be leaps and bounds easier than trying to meet with Yara in the next twenty minutes.

After departing the plane, the freezing wind chills my bones instantly and we hurry to get inside our car waiting on the tarmac. Once we close the door, the heated interior is welcoming but very warm so we remove our gloves and coats, making ourselves comfortable for the trip to the hotel. A few minutes later, our luggage is loaded and we are finally ready to go. As we hit the road, I can't help but look out of my window to take in as much of the landscape as possible. The field on which the airport was built is surrounded on all sides by the Alps, and there's so much to look at as we go that I have a hard time keeping up.

St. Moritz is clearly a town that caters to the wealthy, with women in ankle length fur coats window shopping outside of luxury boutiques. All the buildings are emblazoned with some sort of flag or sign advertising the snow polo tournament, and the festivities for the event seem to have overtaken the town.

The roads aren't too busy, since one game has already started, and it doesn't take us much time at all to get to the hotel. Except, it looks less like a hotel and more like a medieval castle, towering above us. I'm no stranger to five-star hotels and resorts, but seeing the age and all the history of this gigantic stone building fills me with joy and excitement to be here. This place already feels special.

As we get inside, the lobby area is just as stunning, wood and marble polished to a reflective shine, and refined woven rugs covering the floor.

"Damn," Emma says, craning her neck to see the place. "Good choice."

"Alex booked it," I tell her, handing my carry-on bag to one employee while we do our check-in. "He's the expert about places to stay in Europe."

Keycards in hands, one of the staff members escorts us to our rooms located beside each other. They face the frozen lake, with huge floor-to-ceiling windows and linens in all shades of cream and gold. I sink onto the mattress and sigh in pleasure. I had just woken up, but I suddenly want to just lay down in the early morning sunshine and doze off.

Emma is still standing, looking out the window at the polo match already in motion. We're too high off the ground, and there's no way to tell which player is which, or even the colors of the team, but it's still affecting her to see the game.

"Yara doesn't play till later," I tell her, and she just nods.

Finally, she says, "I'm going to go to my room to unpack and shower. I'll come get you right before the match starts. Does that sound alright?"

Mentally, I relax, knowing I'd have time to sneak away and talk to Yara. "That's fine. I'll see you in a bit."

Afraid that I won't have time later, I shower as fast as I can, which is a shame in such an amazing bathroom, rapidly braiding my hair when I get out and throwing my clothes on. I have a dress more suited for the party this evening, but for now, a pair of dark jeans and an ivory cable-knit sweater will do.

I text Yara, and true to her word, there is a car waiting for me outside of the hotel. The driver doesn't say a word to me, just peeks into the rearview mirror to confirm my identity before pulling out of the parking lot to head toward Yara's home.

Like most of her family and her in-laws, Mrs. Van Lawick owns multiple residences around Europe, and she had chosen this one specifically because of these annual snow polo tournaments. According to what Alex told me in Aspen, rumor has it that Yara always has a young woman staying with her at her property. And while Yara is just as hard-nosed and unyielding off the field, it seems like she has let her guard down a few times when it comes to her female companions. Thanks to Margaret though, nothing about Yara's private life pops up in a Google search. At least not in the first few pages. Well, all I can hope is that it stays that way.

As we cross the gates and drive onto her property, I look out of the window, taking in my surroundings. Her outdoors is spacious, but the defining feature is the gigantic patio overlooking the valley where a few employees are setting out ambient heaters, tables, and chairs. This must be where she will hold her own celebration on Sunday if her team comes out on top.

Once the car stops in front of the entrance, the silent driver opens the door for me and escorts me inside. I take a second at the doorstep, straightening my posture and raising my chin. Yara isn't going to intimidate me; not today.

As I observe the hallway, the interior design is minimalist, ultra-modern, with high ceilings, long boards, and veneer applications. And yet, despite the best architecture money can buy, it feels cold and empty. To my surprise, the driver invites me inside what seems to be an open kitchen and dining room, with glass walls giving way to the bright snowy outdoors. I find Yara standing there, looking out of the floor-to-ceiling window, already dressed in her uniform, tall brown riding boots reaching her knees and her long, straight hair caught in a ponytail that hangs down her back. She's not wearing her team's jersey just yet, just a white compression shirt that shows off the lines of her toned arms and stomach. She turns to face me, a freezing smile on her face. I don't say a word, and she doesn't say anything either. She slowly paces across the room, and then goes and sits at a glass dining table, a frosted glass of water in front of her. She remains just as quiet, looking at it as if she's pondering her existence. I know better though. It's all an act to get me to let my guard down.

"Yara," I say simply as I walk over, declining her invitation to sit when she waves a distracted hand at the chair across from her.

"Petra," she responds. "I'm glad you were able to take a break from your babysitting duties and join me."

I sneer but don't rise to her bait. "So, what do you want?"

She runs her finger along the rim of her glass, finally deciding to meet me in the eye. Damn. She looks so similar to Alex that I physically recoil before catching myself.

"I've been thinking, and putting some puzzle pieces together in my mind, and I've come up with a hypothesis about this Japanese woman that seems to be a thorn in my side all of a sudden. Would you like to hear my theory?"

Not really. "Sure, go ahead."

"I think," Yara says seriously, but with a conspiratorial tone in her voice, as if she's telling me a secret, "that *you* are the reason Shiori and Emma are spending so much time together."

Uh-oh. If Yara has busted me and my plan already, why was I even here in Switzerland?

"That's ridiculous," I bluff. "Can I go back to the hotel now? I'm jet lagged."

"Now, let me finish," Yara says, waving a finger at me. She stands, pacing around her open concept kitchen, and I circle at the same time, keeping the counter between us. "It all just makes too much sense. You open your paltry excuse for a gallery right before Shiori's private auction, hoping to drum up an invitation, and low and behold, you get one. Somehow, probably by offering up a boatload of my brother's money, you got the ear of Shiori Takahashi herself and bought her out, on the condition that she flirt it up with Emma."

Yara clenches her teeth upon hearing Emma's name, as if having to admit that Emma was hitting it off with someone else burned her tongue. She then continues, "That would explain why publicly, you won the bid for two paintings, but rumor has it that *eight* of them were delivered to your gallery. It all just seems a little suspicious to me. If anyone was going to use a world-famous artist as a honey trap, it would be you, Petra, you snake."

"Excuse me?" I blurt out, flabbergasted. "What did you just call me?"

"A snake," Yara says again, getting closer and closer to me. "Do you deny it? Trying to hook Shi and Emma up?"

"Yes, I deny it!" I exclaim. "But do you know what? I like them together. They look good. Happy. Not hiding under a rock from anyone's *husband*."

Yara is fast, like the cobra she accuses me of being, and before I can blink, she's toe to toe with me, my butt pressed against her kitchen island as she bares her perfect white teeth in my face, expression contorted with rage. It reminds me of our face-to-face at the Breitner House in Amsterdam and how uncomfortable I felt.

"You," she seethes, "need to mind your own business, little girl. You might have spread your legs and given my brother some children, but you're not family, and you never will be. You're just angry that I'm taking Emma from you, but guess what? She *wants* to come with me. She'd rather be my lover than alone."

She's really pushing my buttons. I've never been a violent person, but the anger she's trying to bring out of me is boiling under my skin, pleading to be released. *Cool down, Petra.* I knew since the day she gripped my wrist at the Breitner House that she was a total psycho. I can feel her breath on my face, and the strength of her slender body radiates. I don't think she will hit me, but it's clear that she really, really wants to. "Get away from me," I demand, my heart pulsing hard in my chest. "Or else—"

"Or else what?"

"I'm gonna report you!" I dare to spit out.

"To who, huh?" She chuckles at me, her head shaking. "My brother isn't here. Emma isn't here. Who are you going to tell that I give a single fuck about?"

I could say the police, but I know they aren't gonna do shit. I smile, thinking something through, which seems to make her even angrier. "The tournament officials," I decide to say instead. "I don't think they'd like it if their star player was roughing up young VIP attendees before matches."

Yara hesitates, before whirling around so fast the edges of her ponytail graze my face. She stomps back to the glass table, taking a swig of her water before wiping her mouth with the back of her hand. She looks me up and down and scoffs.

"You aren't worth any more of my time. Leave. And if I find out you're lying about being behind Shiori and Emma's meeting, you'll live to regret it. Understand?"

I'm full of adrenaline from having her square up to me, and I have to concentrate hard to keep my voice even. "Whatever, Yara." I don't waste my time any longer and turn around just as fast to leave the kitchen and this place altogether.

The taciturn driver is waiting for me again outside, and I consider calling my own car but decide that if Yara wanted to get rid of me permanently, she'd have a more creative idea than having her driver crash us into a ditch.

Our exchange had taken less than fifteen minutes, less time than it had taken to drive to her villa from the hotel, but it leaves me shaken, nonetheless. Yara seems like a pot about to boil over. She's been aggressive with me before, but never on such a short fuse, and never to the point where I actually thought she would lay her hands on me. Either something with her personal life or the polo team is going on, or this thing with Emma is actually bothering her. Is she that controlling? Damn… I truly hope Emma will ditch her once and for all.

I get into the car and the silent driver takes me away once and for all from this witch. All I can hope is that I won't have to come back here any time soon. I take a few deep breaths in and out, trying to relax, but our conversation doesn't stop replaying in my head. I consider giving Alex a call upon my arrival at the hotel and telling him what just happened, but there's the slim chance he'd show up at my hotel door in nine hours, ready to avenge me against his sister, and that doesn't fit in at all with my plans.

A few minutes later, the castle-like hotel finally comes into view and I'm relieved. Oh thank God! My heartbeat is still pounding anxiously fast inside my chest and while I try to appear calm and serene, as soon as the valet opens the door for me, I leap off of my seat, storming through the hallway and then disappear into the lift. Glancing at my watch, I realize I'd be back in plenty of time for a power nap, but I don't think my nerves are going to let it happen. When I get back to my room, I sit on the edge of my bed for a moment to breathe, then take a bottle of chilled water from the mini fridge and roll it over the back of my neck, trying to relieve the tension headache I can feel coming on.

With my iPhone in hand, I check my inbox; nothing from Shiori, and I bite my lip. If she doesn't show up, this ordeal is going to be significantly more difficult. Jeez, how am I supposed to separate Emma from Yara if Shiori doesn't show up? I need a backup plan, just in case. I ruminate a bit, and as I remind myself of the talk we had on the plane, I finally come up with an idea.

The time zone difference makes it tricky, but I send out a text to Matt anyway, hoping that he has some spare time to help an old friend out. He might deny it, but Matt loves a good bit of drama as long as it doesn't involve him.

*Hey, Matt, can you do me a favor pls? I need anything *interesting* regarding Yara and Elliot Van Lawick that Margaret may have scrubbed from the tabloids. Any throwaway stories I might have missed?*

He doesn't respond right away, so with some time to spare, I try to do a little digging on my own, turning up nothing but article after article about Yara's polo team. I need something more personal that could dissuade Emma once and for all to continue with this affair. Maybe something about the other young girls Yara brought here? But then, Matt responds with a link.

Like this?

It's a Google archives link for a webpage that's no longer up, but that Matt could see the history of. I click on it, and the archived page is painfully slow to load, but finally, the one-year-old tabloid headline pops up.

Baby blues? Sources say the Van Lawicks are trying for another child, but is Yara's polo career impeding parenthood bliss?

I read the article so fast that I have to go back and read it again, slower, so I can actually retain what I'm seeing. The article says that one year ago, Yara and Elliot were supposedly heard discussing the possibility of having another child when leaving the doctor's office near their principal family home. Yara had been heard saying she wanted to pursue her polo career but had told her husband they could stop using protection and whatever happened, happened. It was a slimy piece of tabloid gossip, no doubt overheard by a hidden paparazzi, but I'll take what I can get.

Yara obviously never got pregnant, but a year ago was relatively soon after the masquerade, which meant that Yara had been actively sleeping with both Elliot *and* Emma, despite telling Emma that her sex life with him was dead.

Thanks, Matt. That's perfect, I text him, and he replies with a thumbs up emoji.

I don't know if this information would completely deter Emma from continuing to try and be with Yara, but I decide to keep it in my back pocket just in case Shiori doesn't come through. I'll have to tell Emma eventually anyway because this isn't something I can keep from my friend, but all in due time.

I lay back on my bed, folding my hands behind my head and smiling up at the chandelier on the ceiling.

But my few moments of peace don't last long, and soon enough, Emma is knocking on the door connecting our adjoining rooms. Since I don't reply, she just invites herself inside, walking towards me.

"Come on, I don't want to miss the opening of the match," she says, trying to encourage me to leave my comfortable bed.

As my eyes alight on her, my lips curve up into a smile; her hair is glossy and her makeup flawless, and no one would ever be able to guess she had just gotten off a nine-hour flight. Emma is, of course, sporting dark colors, with knee-high black boots and a long gunmetal gray parka lined with black faux fur on the collar and hood.

"Have you talked to her at all?" I ask, curious if Yara had even bothered to speak to her between getting ready for the match and threatening me.

Emma's expression falters. "She texted me her address, but nothing else. I'm sure she's busy, being the team captain and all."

I hold my tongue, wanting to tell her about my earlier visit with my sister-in-law, but knowing that it would just cause unnecessary tension between us. Oh well, I'm excited about the match, even if I have to watch someone I despise playing. It's hard not to get caught up in the place's energy.

Winter wear and veganism aren't the easiest combination to deal with, but my full length faux sable fur coat looks better than expected when I slip it over my shoulders, looking myself over in the mirror. The Snow Polo World Cup may seemingly be primarily about the polo itself, but similar to the Kentucky Derby back stateside, fashion for the onlookers is also key to the event. Instead of stunning gowns and tailored tuxedos, designers provided celebrity attendees with the finest in winter coats, hats, and boots. It had been a scramble to come up with an ensemble for the weekend on short notice, but thanks to Emma, I had acquired a few brilliant vegan-friendly options from her favorite brands.

"Are you ready?" she complains, tapping her foot impatiently as I gather the rest of my things.

I glare, but I am finally ready. I cinch my hood around my face and follow her out of the room. It's ridiculously cold out, but we're dressed for success at least.

***

The polo game is a flurry of activity and excitement, and even if I detest who is playing, I have to admit it's a fun time. The surrounding air is crispy and cold, and while there are heated tents we can retreat to when it becomes too chilly to bear, Emma insists on staying as close as she can to the action, leaning over the railing and cheering on Yara and her team as they take the field.

This match will be Badrutt's Palace Hotel vs. Azerbaijan, but it's clear team Badrutt is the favorite to win. Yara isn't the first woman to play in the world cup, but her fame and fortune have put her in the spotlight more than any other woman on this field before, and all eyes are on her.

I have to admit, she looks impressive, leading her team out onto the frozen lake on her powerful chestnut mount. Hot breath curls from all the horses' nostrils, rising into the air along with the shouts of everyone in the stands. It's so bright from the sun reflecting off the snow that I have to squint to see even with sunglasses on.

The noise around us grows and grows. The cheers and jeers of onlookers combined with the announcers over the loudspeakers and the pounding of the horses' hooves on the snowy ground all converge into one low roar. Emma has us pressed so close up against the barrier that I feel like if I reached my arm out far enough, I could touch the sleek coats of the thoroughbreds.

Emma is almost quivering with excitement, looking with awe at Yara, and I realize then why it will take someone truly extraordinary to separate them. It's because Yara, as much of a terrible person as she is, is also extraordinary. She's gorgeous, confident, strong, and an incredible athlete. It's no wonder she has such a hold over my friend.

Yara's eyes slide over us as she passes, waving to the crowd as they announce her name, but only looking at the two of us. Her expression is steely, her eyes burning through me like hot coals. This is her battlefield, where she feels most powerful, and I am at a distinct disadvantage if I want to go toe-to-toe with her.

Jeez, I really wish Shiori had shown up already.

"They're about to start!" Emma tells me over the din, grabbing onto my sleeve excitedly.

I look longingly at the heated tent behind us before resigning myself to freezing while we watch the match, up close and personal. *There are only four more after this*, I remind myself with an internal groan.

And without further ado, the game begins.

***

I try to stick it out, I really do, but the game stretches over two hours, and I have to steal away a few moments to warm myself in the heated tent. It's not that the game isn't engaging, because I found myself invested in the match right away, swept up by the energy of everyone around us. But I can only take so much cold, so I tear myself away from Emma's side to take a break.

I peel off my gloves, rubbing my reddened hands together and blowing into them to try and disperse the chill before reaching into my bag and checking my phone. Nothing from Shiori, but plenty of baby pictures from Alex that bring a smile to my face.

The ambient heaters in the tent are almost intoxicating, and I find myself seated underneath one, watching the game on a screen instead of outside next to Emma. If I'm being honest, it hurts my heart a little to see how zealous she is to cheer her on. Yara is like an Amazonian warrior on her horse, giving no mercy to the other team, and she completely enraptured Emma. The thoughts of Margaret and the sex tape keep replaying in my mind, and I get a sinking feeling in my stomach. As much as Emma had claimed to be on the fence about her fling with my sister-in-law, she seems a lot more willing to be with her now that they are in the same country. This isn't looking good so far.

"Now that's a surprise," I hear a male voice saying beside me.

His voice sounds familiar, and as I look to my right, my heart drops as I recognize the man standing there.

"You!" I snap at Kenneth, the reporter from RTN who interviewed me at my mom's funeral and then sold an edited version of my interview to the American media. "What are you doing here?"

"I got a media pass," he answers serenely, showing me his badge hanging on his chest. "What brought *you* here?"

I don't want to reply. Actually I want to ignore him as much as I can but he's standing right next to me and the last thing I need is this reporter on my feet. "Well, my sister-in-law is playing so I came here to support her."

"Wow," he utters, sounding impressed. "That's very kind of you to have left your infant twins at home to come here. You must be very close to her."

I can nearly taste the sarcasm in his tone, but I decide to smile and play along. "We are quite close, yes."

Our attention switches to the cheering noises coming from the TV that is broadcasting the match live. The camera is zooming on the crowd and on Emma in particular who seems the most devoted cheerleader.

"Oh, I see you didn't come alone," Kenneth ventures, a smirk playing on his lips. "I didn't know your best friend loved polo so much."

Glancing at the screen, I'm mildly embarrassed at Emma's behavior, and I don't think she realizes how much her enthusiasm is out of touch with the rest of the crowd.

"Yeah, she loves sports," I say, putting on a blasé attitude. "Well, I'm gonna go. Enjoy your time in St. Moritz."

"You too." Kenneth bows his head slightly, but before I can turn my back on him, he calls my name and then says, "Tell your friend to be more discreet."

I swallow dry at his words, and I'm left totally in shock at his "advice." Does he know about their affair? Oh gosh! Maybe that's why he's here! The last thing I need is a new scandal in the media about Emma and Yara for the world to see. I give him a small smile and a nod of the head, before turning around and making my way out of the tent.

I hurry to rejoin Emma outside, finally deciding to demand that we get a seat in the VIP section of the stands instead of standing on the barrier the whole time, but when I work up the energy to go back to find Emma, she's gone. Worried, I walk the length of the barrier looking for her, but when she's nowhere to be found, I check my phone, only to find a message from her.

Yara's valet came to invite me back to her personal viewing box. I'll catch up with you later.

Annoyed, I type a few different scathing messages before deleting them and finally send back a terse *OK, but be discreet* before pocketing my phone again. I'm fuming. I don't want to watch the game alone, or at all really, especially while Emma is waiting like some pet lap dog for Yara to come off the field and give her a few absentminded pats. I kick at the snow with my boot, earning myself a scowl from some people next to me. Shit.

It may be childish, but I decide not to stay for the rest of the game. There is an opening day charity dinner later tonight that I'm expected to attend, but for the moment, I have no desire to bump elbows with these strangers watching my enemy dominate the opposing polo team. I hate that Emma has left me in the dust and I hate even more the fact that Yara is behind it.

Feeling a bit forlorn, I call the driver, pushing through the crowds of coat-clad polo fans until I can slide into the heated car with a sigh of relief.

"Just you, Ms. Van Gatt?" the driver asks, looking around for Emma.

"Yes, Ms. Hasenfratz will join me later," I confirm, a note of bitterness in my voice.

"Very well," the driver says.

Back at the hotel, I send Emma a message letting her know I'm in my room before pinning my hair up and running a hot bath in the deep, sunken jacuzzi tub. I find the novel I had been reading in my carry-on bag and take it with me to the bath, turning on the bubbling jets and slipping beneath the toasty water. Cracking open the book, I recline in the bath and sigh. If I was going to get ditched, I was at least going to enjoy myself.

***

As I'm getting myself ready, I hear stirrings from the adjoining room, but when I open the door to check, expecting to find Emma, I find Yara's valet instead, there to collect Emma's attire for the evening. With clenched teeth, I help him find what he's looking for and send him on his way, resigned to having to go to dinner alone. Damn. I know she came here to be with Yara, but I never thought she'd leave me hanging like an old sock.

The charity dinner is being held in the primary ballroom at the Badrutt Palace, so I don't have to travel far. It's a sprawling space with high, vaulted ceilings and a myriad of tables dotted throughout. Six tables are placed at the front of the room on an elevated platform for the six teams and their families, while I am placed at one of the normal tables.

"Oh, you must be Petra Van Gatt, aren't you?" the woman standing in front of me asks. She seems to be in her mid-forties, sporting a long dark-blue dress with sleeves, short blonde hair, and a pair of glasses. "I'm Fiona Van Lawick, Yara's sister-in-law."

Holy shit! I can't believe this! I do my best not to look too astonished as I shake her hand before she pulls me closer for a three cheek kiss.

"Oh, very nice to meet you, Fiona," I manage to say with a composed smile. "I didn't know Elliot had a sister. You also came all the way from the Netherlands?"

"I actually live in Zurich so I decided to pop over for the tournament."

I nod politely as she talks, wondering if she took this decision deliberately or if it's Yara herself who invited her. Knowing Yara as I do, I've got the feeling Fiona's presence isn't really welcomed here.

"Are you seated at Yara's table?" she asks.

"I'm afraid not," I tell her, feeling slightly embarrassed at my negative answer. "I have a seat at one of the tables close by."

"Oh, perfect. Me too," she answers in excitement.

My eyes widen in surprise. "Really?"

"Yes, I replied to the invitation very last minute and her table was already full."

Despite Fiona's smile and bubbly tone, I have the feeling Yara truthfully didn't bother to accommodate a space for her at her table. As I come to think of it, maybe Emma's right, maybe there are some marital problems going on between Yara and Elliot. The fact Emma is at Yara's table, but not her own sister-in-law will most likely feed the rumor mill. Talking about rumor mill, my gaze zooms at the man standing a few feet away from us talking to another man who's holding a camera. Yep, Kenneth, the reporter from RTL, is here too and I'm pretty sure he's on the hunt for some juicy story about Yara.

"Maybe we are at the same table?" Fiona comments. My attention returns to her, and I suggest we go and check the table chart.

I rejoice when I see my name at her table—at least I won't be spending the dinner alone.

As we walk towards our table, Fiona seems to know quite a few of the people attending the charity dinner tonight. She stops once more to greet another couple and makes sure to introduce me to them. I'm quite surprised at how much she knows about me, my new gallery, and my art fund.

"How come you know so much about me?"

"Oh, I'm an art finance advisor at Deloitte," she explains. "We advise art dealers and collectors, so your gallery and the purchases you did at Christie's came up on our radar."

My brows rise in astonishment. "Wow," I say, still processing the news. "What a great coincidence!"

And just like that, it feels like my evening is going to be much more interesting than I thought.

We finally get to our table after a few more rounds of small talk, which is already full except for our two seats. Fiona doesn't waste time introducing me to all those she knows, and

I must say, her kindness is so refreshing compared to Yara's. Although I won't be sitting beside Emma, I'm at least surrounded by people who know my sister-in-law and the Van Lawicks very well, and I can hold a conversation with them.

Flickering candlelight and crispy white linens greet me as I find my seat, and Fiona's acquaintances welcome me warmly.

I can see Emma at one of the head tables at Yara's side, neither of them touching in any way that would alert the surrounding people they are having an affair, but close enough that Yara could keep an eye on her. Every time I look in that direction, trying to catch Emma's attention, it's Yara gazing back at me instead, a wicked gleam in her eyes and a Cheshire grin on her face. She knows I'm pissed, and after our confrontation earlier today, she isn't going to give me any leeway.

Come back to the hotel tonight, I text Emma. *You can't make an unbiased decision about staying with Yara if you're around her constantly.*

I see Emma check her phone from across the ballroom, and she frowns, looking torn, before texting back:

I came all this way to see her. I might as well spend my time in her company.

I waste no time to reply, *I thought you were excited that the two of us would be traveling alone together again.*

A few seconds later, I receive one more text from her: *And I am! We'll see each other tomorrow at the games. X*

I sit my phone down on the table, blowing out a frustrated breath. Emma is a lost cause, at least for tonight. She needs to get seeing Yara out of her system, and then maybe she would be able to think a little clearer tomorrow.

I'm still holding out hope that Shi appears, but every hour that passes without her here makes me more and more nervous. I have the trump card of the article Matt found, but it isn't going to be nearly as powerful in separating Yara and Emma as Shiori's presence would be.

Ugh. Well, Fiona did me the favor of introducing me to her acquaintances. I might as well spend my time on something useful instead of obsessing over something I can't control. When the conversation around the table lulls, I jump in, more than ready to take my mind off of other people's love lives.

Leaning forward, I clear my throat to get everyone's attention.

"So, has Yara told all of you about my newest art fund that will provide grants for promising new artists? Well, it's called the Gatt-Dieren Art Fund, and we're planning quite a few big events this year at our gallery to raise money. Of course, you'll all be invited..."

***

"How come your brother isn't here?" I finally decide to ask Fiona. After all, we've spent the whole evening getting to know each other, dinner is officially over, and we are the only two left at our table.

Fiona gives me a small smile in return, before finishing her champagne. "Elliot never attends her tournaments," she says. "And I don't think Yara would like him here anyway."

"Really?" I ask, genuinely surprised at her answer. "But why not? It's her husband, after all."

Fiona doesn't hide her uneasiness at my questioning. She remains silent for a few instants, considering me. "Well, according to what my brother told me, she doesn't want him at her place of work." She pauses as if she's pondering whether to add something else or not. "And I think he is okay with that."

"So she invited you but not her brother?" The question instantly rolls off my tongue, likely due to my indulgence in champagne, and I find myself already regretting it.

Fiona shifts in her seat, smiling unpleasantly at me, and I wonder if I crossed some boundary. "I'm sorry I was just—"

"Oh, that's okay," she interposes, cutting me off. "Yara didn't invite me." The sadness in her tone is overly palpable and it squeezes my heart to see her like this. "Do you remember the couple who was seated here?" she asks, pointing at the two empty seats on her right.

I nod.

"They are the ones who did." Her features deepen and she lets out a sigh, her gaze falling to her lap. "To be honest, I came here to see if what I had read online was true."

My curiosity is perked. "What did you read online?"

Fiona sneers, shaking her head briefly. "I'm afraid that's something really private."

"I understand," I say, forcing myself to smile.

Despite the secrecy, I remember what Alex told me about the young women who used to come and stay at Yara's place. If Fiona came here to find out the truth about them, then Emma might end up on her radar. I look up at the head table, but Emma isn't there anymore. Yara, on the other hand, is taking some pictures with her team and sponsors. I scan across the ballroom and tables, but I don't see Emma anywhere. *Where on earth is she*?

Standing up, I take my clutch, and say, "Well, I'm gonna go and get some sleep."

After bidding farewell to Fiona, I leave the ballroom, marching towards the lift.

After reaching my bedroom, I open the door that gives access to the adjacent room and find it totally empty.

Emma told me she wasn't gonna sleep here, but I was still hoping otherwise. I take my iPhone and decide to call her. A few ringtones go on until I finally hear her voice.

"Hey, where are you?" I ask, my voice is sweet but worried. "Is everything alright?"

"Yeah, um, I'm at her place," she answers. "It's pretty dope. She's got a huge jacuzzi on her balcony."

"Emma, please be discreet," I say, my tone coming off more fearful than I'd wanted. "I was seated next to Elliot's sister, and believe me, she didn't come here for the polo games."

"I know, that's why I left early." Her tone, on the other hand, is totally chill. "Don't worry, I'm gonna be okay."

As I pay attention to the gurgling sound coming from the other side of the line, I can picture the bubbly water flowing in the hot tub. "Are you in her jacuzzi right now?"

"Yep, it's pretty relaxing."

"Please, be careful," I repeat, my nerves rising up. "Don't give the paparazzi what they want."

"Oh, jeez, I know," she answers in annoyance. "We'll speak tomorrow, alright?"

I sigh, both displeased and disappointed at her behavior. "Fine. See you tomorrow."

After we hang up, I go to bed, my mind ruminating non-stop. I must say, I never thought it'd be so damn hard to separate those two.

CHAPTER 9

St. Moritz, January 29, 2022
Petra

"When are you going to stop being pissed at me?" Emma asks, elbowing me.

I blow out a breath, pulling my coat tighter around my body as I try to fight the cold wind chilling my bones. "I'm not pissed."

"Don't lie to me," Emma insists. "I know you better than that."

I look at the member of the staff who is trying to fix the heater that stopped working a few minutes ago and then at Emma again. "I just hate that you couldn't even hold off a single night before going to stay with her."

"Come on!" she snaps, feigning outrage. "You knew the whole reason I was coming was to see her. You can't be mad that I spent time with her."

"I know. I'm just worried," I confess, and Emma gives me a quick side hug, even when I try to brush her off.

"I know you are," she says in a whisper, squeezing me. "But you don't have to worry about me so much."

That's where you're wrong, I think, but keep silent, just untangling myself from Emma's embrace.

"The heater is all fixed," the man announces proudly.

"Ah, thank you so much!" I stand up from my seat and put my hands as close to the fire as possible. Despite being in the VIP section of the stands, we aren't much more protected from the cold, but at least we have a heater right beside us.

The second game of the day has just ended, and it's becoming clear to everyone at the tournament that Yara's team is going to be the winner of the competition. As much as I hate seeing Yara succeed, her constant victories mean she has been kept busy most of the day with interviewers and sponsors, so Emma has stuck with me instead of watching the games from Yara's private viewing box alone.

Emma did a walk of shame early this morning, and when I woke up, I found the door between our rooms shut. When I cracked it open for a peek, I saw her buried under the covers of her bed, snoozing in the early light. She must have had a busy night. Yuck.

A few hours later, she had knocked quietly on our connecting door before letting herself in, her arms full of a bag of bagels and a drink holder full of coffees. "Good morning," she had said in a guilty voice, begging me with her eyes not to ask further questions.

I had been dying to know what exactly had happened last night, but from her face and body language, I knew she didn't want to talk to me about it. I let it slide, and we had a tense breakfast in my room before going to the first game.

Now, it's getting dark, and we have very little time to get ready for the cocktail party being held at the ballroom of the opulent Kulm Hotel. Despite the fact that Yara has her final match tomorrow afternoon, all the polo players including herself will be present, so obviously, Emma doesn't want to miss out on the social event.

And frankly, neither do I.

I'm swiftly running out of time to persuade Emma to separate from Yara on her own accord. All I can hope is that Yara will snub Emma tonight, afraid of the paparazzi taking pictures of the two of them together and exposing their affair. No red flags had gone up in the media yet, but the closer Yara gets to the championship cup, the more popular she is with all the reporters and photographers. As of right now, she's the media darling of the Snow Polo World Cup, and any little thing she does or says is reported on.

Once we get back to the hotel room, we help each other get ready for the cocktail party, just like old times. I slick my hair back from my face, letting it hang stick-straight down my back while Emma fluffs her signature bob. I've gone with a taupe wrap dress and Emma is wearing a more modern black and silver designer suit.

After an all-too-brief FaceTime conversation with my husband and the twins, Emma and I are finally ready to go. The swift change from talking to my children to falling right back into the mold of a socialite feels strange like I shouldn't be here tonight but in Manhattan, home with my family.

Emma, on the other hand, seems to be perfectly fine and even excited about tonight.

As we cross the lobby area of the hotel, I notice her one-piece ensemble clings to the curves of her body almost scandalously, and her heels are so high that she's almost two full inches taller than I am. We both look ready for the red carpet, but I know it will be her that the cameras will truly adore.

Unlike the night before, there's no assigned seating, but there is a red-carpet entryway where the media is camped out to talk to players and other famous attendees. We exit the car, my heart already racing, and as we walk towards the entrance, some photographers shout for us to stop and strike a pose. We put on our best behavior and let them have our photo taken, whether or not we wanted to.

If the energy at the games was frenzied, it is pulsing in an entirely different way here at the cocktail party. The strict rules of the games had disappeared, and players were now mingling with models and influencers, all of them posing for pictures with wide smiles and sultry pouts on their faces. The lounge music is not too loud, allowing people to form groups and strike up conversations. It reminds me of the dinner parties my dad used to host, and as I take in my surroundings, guests seem to have only three things in mind: look good, make conversation, and drink a lot.

After smiling and greeting all the faces I recognize, I immediately head to the bar to order a drink. To my surprise, Emma excuses herself while I do so, and by the time I have my glass in hand, she is long gone. I tap my nails against my glass of bubbly, scanning the room for her.

"Are you looking for someone?"

I turn to my left side, following the female voice, and my gaze alights on Fiona, a Martini in hand, a beautiful smile gracing her glossy lips.

I decide to be honest with her, so I reply accordingly. "Actually, yes, Emma, my best friend who came here with me."

"Oh, with the amount of beautiful men here, I'm sure she's already busy."

I wet my lips with the champagne, left totally speechless at her comment. I'm at least relieved to know Fiona hasn't a clue as to who Emma is.

"Are you enjoying the games?" I decide to ask in order to change the subject.

For some reason, her smile turns into a smirk, and after taking a sip from her Martini, she says, "I didn't come here for the games, Petra."

"Oh, okay," I utter, trying to hide my discomfort. If Fiona came here to find out if her sister-in-law is having an affair, then I should make sure Emma spends the evening on her best behavior. I survey again across the room, my attention landing on the flashes and noises coming from the entrance.

Yara makes her way in, sporting her polo uniform, and is immediately swamped by cameras and reporters wanting to know how she is feeling the night before the championships. She ignores them and crosses the room to join the rest of her team, passing through Emma as she does so, who recognizes her instantly. Yara, on the other hand, ignores her like she's part of the media, not even bothering to acknowledge her presence. I notice how crushed Emma looks, even if she does her best to keep her composure and poker face while she walks back toward the bar to get a drink of her own. To my surprise, she doesn't stop by my side. Instead, she goes all the way to the end of the bar and sits on a stool, alone. Damn. She must feel terrible inside.

"We haven't spoken since I arrived," Fiona discloses, her eyes on Yara, who is now opening a bottle of Dom Perignon with her team and her sponsors. Fiona's tone is unusually serious, filled with sadness that wasn't there a minute ago.

"Don't worry," I answer, giving a soft pat on her arm. "If it helps, Yara hasn't said a word to me either."

Fiona is talking to me when she suddenly looks over my shoulder, stopping her sentence mid-syllable. "Holy shit," she says, her eyes pinned behind me. "Is that who I think it is?"

Curious, I turn to see who had entered, right as the crowd explodes in excited chatter, camera flashes light up the room.

Flanked once more by her enormous bodyguard and her personal assistant, Shiori Takahashi enters the cocktail party, wearing a floor-length red sheath dress with black vine designs climbing up the front, and a pair of small-lensed sunglasses.

Everyone in the room suddenly looks at her, people exclaiming in surprise at her entrance. No one in this room seems to be a stranger to the young Japanese painter who had just sold a fifteen million dollar portrait back in New York, and it wasn't lost on anyone either that the person who had purchased said painting was also in attendance.

I can't hide my smile, pushing past the stuttering Fiona to find Emma.

Yet her stool at the bar is empty, and as I turn around, I find her standing motionless halfway between where I am and where Shiori is standing. I can see her eyes are wide, locked on Shi, who is looking right back at her, a lazy smile on her red-painted mouth.

I shove onlookers out of the way until I reach Emma, grabbing her arm. "Oh my God! I had no idea she was coming!" I lie straight through my teeth.

Emma shoots me a quick glance and swallows. "Yeah, me neither," she says, just loud enough to be heard over all the other voices. "What are the fucking chances…"

"Emma!" I exclaim. "She's looking right at you! Why are you just standing there?"

Emma looks behind us, and I follow her gaze, seeing what has made her hesitate to go to Shiori. Yara is standing, tall and proud, with her arms crossed, glaring directly at Shiori. Her eyes are shooting daggers, and if looks could kill, Shiori would be in trouble.

"Emma," I say again. "Who cares? Go. See. Shi." I give her a not-so-gentle push towards the entryway, and after a stuttering step, she turns her head away from Yara and walks almost mechanically to Shiori.

I follow in her wake, not wanting to miss whatever is going to happen between the two of them. Shi pushes her glasses up as Emma approaches before she holds both her hands out. Emma reaches her hands out too until Shiori is gently holding both of Emma's hands and smiling at her with surprising softness.

"Emma," Shiori purrs. "It seems like the universe has brought us together once again. What luck."

The press is going *insane*, cameras snapping so rapidly I can barely hear myself think. From my peripheral, I can see Yara pushing through the crowd toward us, but no one seems to want to move for her. Everyone is too fixated on this new turn of events.

"I can't believe you're here," Emma breathes, and I see her smile reach her eyes for the first time since we've landed in Switzerland.

"Come, show me around. I've only just landed and came straight here," Shi says, waving her hand around the party. Emma seems ready to agree, but at that moment, Yara has finally made her way toward us.

Yara is taller than both Shiori and Emma, and she looks down at them disdainfully, a slight sneer pulling at her lips. She, just like the rest of the polo players, is still in uniform, and she radiates power. "I don't believe we've met," she tells Shiori with mock interest. "I'm Yara Van Lawick, captain of the Badrutt's Palace Hotel team. And you are?"

People around us murmur in disbelief that Yara doesn't know who Shi is, wondering why the captain of the winning team would be rude to such a famous artist visiting her team's hometown for the first time. Shiori is no stranger to shady comments though and fires right back.

She lets go of Emma's hands and approaches Yara until they are standing just a few inches apart. She looks up at the older woman fearlessly, only mild curiosity in her expression. "Shiori Takahashi. Yes, I think I've heard of you. You're Elliot Van Lawick's wife, right?" I can see Yara's jaw working at the mention of her husband, but Shiori isn't quite finished. "Oh, and Petra's sister-in-law, correct? Yes, yes, I recognize the name. I'll soon have work on display at Petra's gallery. I'm sure you've heard."

Shiori's response might seem innocuous, but in just a few words she has relegated Yara, the captain of the current winning team, to a wife and my sister-in-law, not mentioning any of Yara's own achievements. Yara is the media's focus at the Snow Polo World Cup, and this sudden shift of attention to Shiori, plus Shiori's nonchalance at not recognizing Yara, has a flush of anger creeping up her neck.

"Seems strange that an artist who was just in New York would show up to a snow polo tournament when she's shown no interest in the sport before," Yara ripostes through a clenched jaw. "Some people may think you're just here for clout."

Shiori is unbothered, shrugging one pale, bare shoulder. "No. Just for the scenery, and I thought my good friend Emma could explain the game to me. Plus, the tournament directors seemed so adamant that I came to St. Moritz. I would have hated to disappoint them."

Yara stands up even straighter, and I can almost see the scathing retorts she wants to spit out. "*Emma won't be showing you shit,*" or *"Enjoy the attention while you can because this is my show and you'll be forgotten soon enough,"* but the media is all around us, and as the captain of team Badrutt's Palace Hotel, she can't be her usual disrespectful self.

Instead, she just gives Shiori a tight nod. "I hope you enjoy the tournament, then. Don't hesitate to ask if you need *anything* while you are here."

Shi, in a show of unbothered confidence, runs the back of her hand down Emma's arm, causing Emma to startle and

Yara's eyelid to twitch. "Oh, I'm sure my dear friends Emma and Petra can help me with anything I'll need. Good luck tomorrow, Mrs. Van Lawick."

Yara whips herself around, returning to where her team is standing, watching the exchange in silence, just like the rest of the party.

Shi's personal assistant comes over and leans towards her, murmuring something in her ear. After a quick talk, Shiori excuses herself from us, saying that she's going to answer a few of the media's questions before joining us again. Emma, a goofy grin on her face, loops her arm over my shoulders, and she says under her breath so only I can hear, "What the fuck is happening right now?"

I pat her on the cheek, responding, "Well, Cinderella, looks like you're the belle of the ball tonight and all the queens want to dance with you."

Emma looks down at her heels, raising one foot up to examine the shining silver metal stiletto. "Do you think if I run and drop a shoe outside, my soulmate will scour the town for me?"

I laugh. "No such luck. You're just going to have to stick it out with me and all the other commoners."

"Well, shit." Emma sighs, closing her eyes. "I hate balls."

***

To my immense satisfaction, Emma comes back to Badrutt's with me after the party, slipping through the throngs of people to covertly get into the car I had called to pick me up, looking both happy and weary.

"I can't bounce between the two of them anymore," she says, sliding down the leather seat in exhaustion. "They're like two lions and I'm the gazelle."

I chuckle, grateful to be alone again. "You know, I always thought *you* would be the lion, not the other way around."

"Yeah, me too," she admits. "I even surprise myself sometimes."

"So," I ask conspiratorially, "what are you going to do tomorrow?"

Emma rubs her face with her hands, groaning. "I don't fucking know. Yara said she expects me in her viewing box during the final game, but Shiori invited us both to *hers*. She says she wants me to explain polo to her." Emma snorts. "I barely understand it myself."

"Maybe it's a euphemism," I say with a giggle.

"Pervert," she retorts, giving me a quick slap on the arm.

We both dissolve into real, relieved laughter, much of the tension of the last twenty-four hours fading away. I'm so glad to have her with me, and she seems more relaxed out of Yara's sphere of influence.

"Well, I'm going to Shiori's tent. I don't know about you," I say once we settle down. "I won't try to influence you one way or the other, but I will say that Shiori is much less likely to throw a tantrum if Yara's team loses."

"I know you're joking," Emma replies. "But she will not lose. She's full of so much fire right now. I don't think anyone could take her team down." I can see her eyes glittering as Emma speaks about Yara. "She leads them with an iron fist, but they all seem to flourish under her." She then nods pensively, a small smile emerging at the corner of her lips.

"Yeah, Yara is gonna take the championship cup, I guarantee it." The enthusiasm and determination in her voice brings me back to the ugly reality—Emma is still very much attached and loyal to Yara, no matter how badly she treated her at the party.

"We'll never hear the end of it from Margaret if she does," I say, trying to compose a smile. "Just another unreachable standard for me."

"Eh, I don't think anyone expects you to be a sports star, Petra," she answers.

"No, but Margaret will take any opportunity to prove that her own flesh and blood are superior to me." I shrug. "I'm used to it by now."

Once we're back at the hotel in the elevator, Emma seems lost in thought, finally announcing, "I'm at least going to go with Shiori for the first game. I don't think I can sit through six hours' worth of polo by myself in the cold."

"Yara's going to be pissed," I mention to tease her.

"Yeah, well, when isn't she?" Emma says with a tired look in her eyes. "I'm used to it by now too."

She unlocks the door to her room, and I follow her inside, planning to just access my room from our adjoining door. Her curtains are wide open, and the bright moonlight illuminates the area just enough that we both see the single potted orchid on Emma's bedside table with a note attached.

I don't have to ask who it's from. Emma picks up the note gingerly, as if it might disintegrate the second she touches it and reads it slowly. I see her throat bob as she swallows and she blinks rapidly, as if clearing her eyes.

"It's a haiku," she says simply, holding the card out for me to read.

I want to see
And to meet you
Stepping on the thin ice.

-Mayuzumi Madoka

"That's so romantic," I breathe, watching as she strokes the orchid's soft white petals. "What are you going to do?"

Emma exhales slowly. "I'm going to go to bed."

I don't really believe her, but I wish her goodnight anyway, clicking the door between our rooms shut behind me. I take another long bath, reading to distract myself from the eventful day. After tomorrow, I will finally go home, and thanks to tonight, there should be enough pictures out there of Emma and Shiori holding hands to convince Margaret that Emma is finally moving on. I might not have actually separated Yara and Emma for sure yet, but Margaret didn't need to know that.

I call Alex as I climb beneath the sheets, filling him in on the day's events and happenings. He's clearly not as invested as I am, but I appreciate being able to tell someone else anyway. We talk about what the twins ate today, some potential candidates for my new personal assistant, and the idea of a graffiti wall at the gallery. If I close my eyes, I can almost pretend Alex is here next to me, and it's a comforting thought.

***

A subtle clicking noise can be heard from the other room which wakes me up just enough to process what the sound could be. Following the click, I hear the quiet footsteps of Emma leaving her hotel room and walking down the carpeted hallway. If I were a betting woman, I'd put good money on Shiori having a room here too.

The thought makes me smile as I drift back to sleep. Stepping on thin ice, indeed.

CHAPTER 10

St. Moritz, January 30, 2022
Petra

There's nothing better than waking up in the morning with a new text message from Alex. I click eagerly on the notification and read his SMS: *Looks like it's getting heated in St. Moritz...*

Below his text, there are a few links that send me to articles in several online publications.

I click on the first one and a few seconds later, a new window opens and I land on a big picture of Emma and Shiori holding hands at the cocktail party yesterday night. Well, it seems like the reporters didn't waste time. A smile spreads up to my ears as I read the headline, "*Shi & Emma, the beginning of a new romance?*"

I scroll down the article which talks in great detail about the cocktail party, including Yara's weird interference, but fortunately, nothing that seems too alarming except the following question, "*Why was Yara Van Lawick, captain of team Badrutt's Palace Hotel, so rude towards Japanese painter Shi?*" Along with a video of the four of us as we listen to Yara's bitchy comments. A huge weight slips off my shoulders as I realize the noise in the background is too loud to hear what Yara is saying. Not surprisingly, the article is signed by nonetheless but Kenneth himself. I click on the other articles and all of them have very similar text and pictures. Well, at least the main focus of the story is not Yara and Emma, but Shiori. As I come to think of it, Emma hasn't spent one single moment alone with Yara at any social event, so it'd have been impossible for the media to snap a picture of the two alone doing anything affectionate—except of course at Yara's villa, but so far nothing has emerged in the media about it.

Well, at least today we will spend the morning at Shi's tent so the media will be able to write even more about the romance between the two, which is absolutely perfect! The more articles about Shi and Emma, the better! I decide to call Alex and thank him for his thoughtful message.

"Good morning, wife." His voice is warm and delicious, melting me to the core. "Did you enjoy the party yesterday? I know someone who looked clearly pissed off."

A quick snort rolls off my mouth. "Yep, I know that one too." With a wistful smile, I glance to my left at the empty pillow and lowering my voice, I say, "What a pity you aren't here. I miss you so much."

"I miss you too," he answers, his voice so caring that it makes me smile. "I can't wait for you to come back home tomorrow."

"I feel so tempted to come back tonight, seriously."

"It's best you make sure Emma comes back all in one piece," he says, his tone shifting from warm to rather serious. "The last thing you need is for her to stay in St. Moritz with my sister after the tournament is over."

Holy shit! I didn't even think about it! "Wait. Do you think Yara will do that?"

"Well, that's what she usually does," Alex tells me. "And that's how she got caught last time."

I remain silent for a moment, considering his words. "It was Kenneth who caught her and published that story, wasn't it?"

"Yep, he's always behind my family digging for some scandal whenever he can."

"Fiona was at the party yesterday," I disclose since I had already told Alex why she had come here. "But so far I don't think she knows anything."

"Be careful with her," he warns. "Fiona has never been fond of my sister. If she can persuade Elliot to get a divorce, all the better for her."

"I know, I know."

I'm about to bid farewell to Alex when my ringtone startles me announcing a new SMS. Checking it out, I notice it's from an unknown number. Well, that's odd, but as curious as I am, I open and read it… Crap! Speak of the devil! "You won't believe who just texted me asking if I already got breakfast."

"Fiona?" he says, a slight worry in his tone.

"It's insane! Why does she want to meet me?" My voice nearly quivers at the end of my sentence, matching my rising heartbeat. "Should I just ignore her text?"

He takes a few seconds to answer, most likely assessing several options. "I think it's best you go. Who knows what she wants? Maybe it's nothing to worry about. Either way, getting to know Fiona can be an advantage."

I nod, agreeing to his advice. I don't need more enemies, and if I don't go, Fiona might even get suspicious.

"Alright, I will reply to her, then," I tell him as I get myself ready to text her back.

"That's my girl," Alex says with his usual humor. "Let me know how it goes."

"I will," I answer promptly, leaping out of bed. "Well, I'm gonna go get ready. Love you."

"Love you too, little Petra. Be careful."

***

My empty stomach is already grueling to the point of being uncomfortable when I reach the breakfast hall. My eyes start zooming at the buffet, salivating at the delicious, warm pastries on display. From the chocolate croissant to the one filled with almonds, I feel like trying them all. But before I can even take a plate and serve myself, I notice from the corner of my eye, a tall woman with short brown hair who stands from her table, a wide smile on her lips.

"Petra," she greets enthusiastically as she walks towards me.

"Oh, Fiona, good morning," I reply, mentally kicking myself for not reaching that croissant I so desperately need.

"Thank you for coming so quickly." She points to the empty chair in front of hers, and says, "Please have a seat."

"Uh…" I glance at the pastries for a moment and then at her. "I will just pick a few things at the buffet first."

"Oh, you can just ask the server to do it for you," she replies, waving a hand to one of them, and she sits back at her table. "Come have a seat."

Noticing the waitress approaching our table, I decide to sit and order the pastries directly from her along with a tea, while trying my best to tame my grueling stomach.

"So," she begins, once our order has been taken and we are both finally alone at our table. "How was yesterday night? It looks like Shi and Emma are, um, a thing?"

My eyes widen in surprise at her blunt question. Wow. She doesn't waste time to get to the point. "Oh, eh, well, that's what the media says but who knows." I try to remain as vague as possible. "They can always make up stories for the sake of it."

"I see…" She nods pensively, before asking, "But is your friend… I mean, into women?"

Why on earth does she want to know that? I shift in my seat, wondering what she's up to.

"Here's the chocolate croissant you ordered and your tea," the waiter announces as she stops at our table.

I clap my hands, looking languorously at my croissant with its little chocolate chips on top, while she pours some tea into my cup.

Once the server leaves, I attack my defenseless croissant, giving a monster bite. I close my eyes, savoring the pastry and forgetting for a moment that Fiona is in front of me posing extremely personal questions about my best friend. Then as I realize something, I look at my croissant and say, "How strange there's no chocolate inside."

Fiona snorts at my observation, leaning closer. "You know what I find strange?" she asks, a malicious smile rising at the corner of her lips.

My heart skips a beat as I watch her gaze fixate on me. I shake my head in response, waiting for her to say the rest.

"The fact your friend Emma went to our sister-in-law's place and spent her first night there." I swallow drily at her comment, most likely unable to hide my embarrassment.

My cheeks must've turned red at her unveiling the truth. I dip my lips to my cup of tea, trying to hide myself behind it. Since Fiona is still sitting in front of me, her eyes observing my every move, I put down the cup, and try to sound as confident as possible. "I understand it can look very suspicious or even weird to you, but I can assure you that whatever she went there for, they are just friends. Emma has known Yara for a few years now, since she's my best friend."

Fiona leans back on her chair as if she's assessing my answer. "Yet it's quite strange your friend arrived at her place one hour before Yara did." I raise an eyebrow at her statement and decide to mimic her position—leaning back on my chair. "It feels like they were trying not to be caught leaving the hotel together."

Fuck… Tension fills the air between us, and it becomes hard to breathe. "And?" I ask, crossing my arms over my chest, unimpressed. "The media makes up stories based on *anything* as I just said, they just wanted to avoid any useless gossip." I bring myself forward and resume eating my croissant which turned out to be very deceptive when it comes to its lack of chocolate. Then to make sure she stops ruminating about Emma spending the night at Yara's, I add, "Honestly, I understand your frustration about our sister-in-law, but Yara and Emma are just friends. That's it. You're just running scenarios in your head."

"Very well," Fiona says as she tries to hide her discontent with a smile, but it's just too obvious. "I'm gonna have to go." She then stands up and takes her purse, putting it across her shoulder. "Thank you for your time." And she finally starts walking away. Suddenly, though, she stops in her tracks, turning around. "Oh, by the way…" She comes a bit closer to me and then asks, "This little chat stays between us, right?"

"Of course," I mechanically answer. "Have a great rest of your day."

She gives me a quick pat on the back before she finally leaves. I heave a sigh of relief, but I'm more than happy to be able to go to that wonderful buffet by myself and find the perfect croissant filled with chocolate.

***

"Why are you yawning?" I ask Emma when she comes through our shared door late in the morning, dressed for the day but yawning so hugely that her jaw cracks.

"Because it's early," she responds.

Despite grinning at the sour look she gives, I glance at my watch before saying, "It's eleven a.m. and we're already late for the first game."

"Yara's only playing in the afternoon," she informs me.

"Yes, but Shiori is waiting for us."

"Alright, let's go then." Emma is already passing through me when I stop her in her tracks. She shoots me an arched brow.

"We have to talk first," I say.

Emma heaves a sigh, crossing her arms over her chest. "What is it?"

"Be discreet," I remind her once more with a stern voice. "I mean, regarding Yara."

"I know!" she snaps in annoyance, and before I can add something more, she grabs my arm, and rushes us out of my bedroom. "C'mon, let's go!"

As we cross the hallway, my mind starts ruminating about the likelihood of Yara staying in St. Moritz for a few more days after the tournament, and I can't help but wonder if Emma is thinking of staying too. Once we get into the lift, it becomes oddly silent while I assess whether or not I should ask her about it. Decided, I arm myself with some courage and turn to Emma. "Can I ask you something else?"

She exhales loudly, her irritation growing. "Sure."

Yet the doors of the elevator open right afterward, so we cross the lobby and get out of the hotel. We find our car parked outside and once we finally get in and sit, I ask, "You are coming back with me to Manhattan tomorrow morning, right?" My gaze is on her, but she simply turns her face to the window, avoiding mine. "Emma?"

She heaves a long sigh, remaining silent for a few seconds. "Yara's staying for a few more days…"

"You're kidding, right?" I snap, totally shocked at her reasoning. "After everything she did to you, you are thinking of staying with her?"

"I don't know yet," she says, her voice small. "I don't know."

A gush of air rolls off my lips at her undecided nature. If Emma stays here with Yara, she's gonna be completely under her influence and will never get rid of her.

I feel the urge to lecture her about how manipulative and controlling Yara is, but what for? Emma already knows that.

"Here we are," she announces when the driver stops in front of the entrance to the tournament. She exits the car just as fast, trying to avoid the subject of her staying longer in St. Moritz.

I try to catch up and resume the conversation, but Emma's already talking to the staff member who was waiting for us to take us to Shi's tent. I exhale the freezing air and follow them in silence. All I hope is that after spending the day with Shi, Emma understands that it's in her own interest to go back to Manhattan.

***

Shiori's tent is not only heated, but she has a small spread of food and a glass carafe of hot green tea that might be the most welcoming sight so far this morning for me. I gratefully pour myself a cup and shed my heavy outer faux fur coat. The tent is warm enough for just my fleece jacket.

Shiori is positively radiant, dressed in a matching black tracksuit and her shimmering hair loose around her heart-shaped face. The look she gives Emma when she walks in behind me says a thousand words, and Emma blushes, quickly shuffling to the refreshment table to busy herself until the redness in her cheeks subsides.

I lean down while Emma is distracted, whispering to Shiori, "I'm so glad you came."

Shi shakes her head, hair dancing in glimmering waves. "It's good for me to step outside of my comfort zone. Think nothing of it."

We both know why she really came here, and it has nothing to do with comfort zones and everything to do with the woman standing behind us filling a small plate with fruit. I take a seat in one of the cushioned lounge chairs, leaving an empty seat between Shiori and me for Emma. We had arrived during one of the minor breaks in the game, and it was getting ready to resume. Whichever team wins this round will go on to face Yara's team in the championships later today. Tension in the air around the teams is palpable and everyone cheers when the players finally come back to the field.

On the sidelines, paparazzi switch between taking pictures of the game and taking pictures of Shiori's tent, no matter how many times her bodyguard shoos them away. They aren't the only ones snapping photos though—phones in the crowd are turned in our direction constantly, trying to get their own picture of the mysterious artist and her confidants.

Emma and Shiori talk softly throughout the match, and midway through I see Shi pull out a sketchbook, drawing absentmindedly as the game goes on. The stands are crowded but not completely filled. Many people are resting up for the championship game later this afternoon.

The one person who is not resting up though, is Yara.

Emma's phone goes off again and again, to the point where it's noticeable to everyone in the tent. We all know who it is, but we all politely ignore it. Yara can't be with Emma, even if Emma wasn't here. She's off preparing her team for their final match, meaning she's only pissed she can't keep tabs on Emma.

Finally, Emma excuses herself to make a phone call at the back of the tent, and I can't help but leave my seat too and go spend an extended amount of time at the refreshment table listening in to the conversation.

"Yara, it's not like that. Yes, I know what it looks like, but isn't it a good thing?"

I can't hear what Yara is saying on the other line, but Emma looks stricken. "It's a good thing because it helps as a cover up! You know what? Whatever. I'm hanging up now."

I try to bolt back to my seat, but Emma catches me, and while I think she's going to scold me for eavesdropping, she waves me over out of earshot of Shiori.

"I don't know what to do," she gushes. "Yara wants the truth, but if I tell her what Shiori and I did last night, she'll never speak to me again."

I'm silent for a moment. "That isn't exactly a bad thing."

"Petra, I'm not ready to let her go." Emma's voice is small, and she looks over at Shiori, who is sketching quietly while the match rages on. "But I don't want to stop seeing Shi, either."

"You already know what I'm gonna say. Shiori is single, unproblematic, and *exactly* your type. More so, she's actually interested in *you*, not just making you follow her arbitrary rules like Yara is."

Emma covers her face with her hands. “I need more time to think,” she says, muffled by her fingers. “This is all too sudden.”

“For right now, just come back and watch the match with us. Nothing is going to get solved in the next few hours, so why not enjoy yourself and stop beating yourself up?”

She still looks uncertain, but after a moment's hesitation, she follows me back to the seats at the front of the tent. Shiori smiles at her as she sits, welcoming her back by taking Emma's hand in her own and lacing their fingers together. Photographers capture the moment like their lives depend on it. And I bet that one of those pictures will be published all over the gossip mags in a few hours. The distressed look on Emma's face melts away, and we all go back to watching the tail end of the semi-final game.

***

The final game is scheduled for two hours after the end of the semi-finals to give the team that just played a chance to rest.

“I'm going back to the hotel,” Shi announces. “Can I give you a ride?”

“Yes, please,” I answer, and I watch Emma with amusement as Shiori confirms that she's staying at the same hotel as us.

“Okay, I'll see you both later on, then,” Emma says, after checking something on her phone.

My eyes squint slightly in surprise. “You aren't coming with us?”

"No, I've got to go to Yara's place and gather the things I left there," she discloses. "I'm hoping there's no one there except her butler since she should be out preparing with her team."

"Alright, be careful, okay?"

I give Emma a quick hug before watching her walk away and get into her black sedan. Then I follow Shi and we get into hers.

We sit beside each other in the back seat and once our doors shut close behind us, the driver turns on the engine and Shi heaves a long sigh. "We haven't had a chance to talk privately," she begins. "How is the setup of the extra pieces I sent you coming along?"

"Oh, amazing, thank you so much to have sent them," I tell her. "We weren't ready for such a large array of pieces, so I've had to do some rearranging." I pull out my phone to show her some photos I had taken of the set of her paintings already set up in the gallery.

"You have a good eye for color, but I'd expect nothing less from a fellow painter," Shiori says as she flips through the pictures. "I hope my works can give your gallery the exposure it needs to thrive."

We talk about the gallery, and Shi gives me some suggestions on how to present her digital pieces to get the best reactions from guests. When the conversation winds down though, the topic shifts to my best friend.

"I'm going to invite her to an exhibition I am having back in Japan," she announces just like that. "I know it's a big step for something so casual, but I think we have a special connection. I feel it in the spaces between her and me." Shiori's voice is wistful.

"I hope she accepts," I tell her. "I think you came into her life both at the right time and the wrong time. She needed you to jolt her out of the fugue she was in regarding Yara, but it isn't fair to you to be interested in someone who has to split their affections."

"Monogamy is not as important to me as honesty and love," Shiori says, and I make a conscious effort to remain as unimpressed as possible. "For the right person, I could be monogamous, but I could never share a lover with someone as toxic as Yara for very long. If Emma can set herself free, I will be there to remind her how to fly."

Wow. She certainly has a way with words. "You're a pretty special person, Shiori."

She smiles, gazing out the window at the towering Alps. "So I've been told."

***

More news stories about Shi and Emma have emerged across the web and I couldn't be happier about it. The fact that they held hands while watching the morning game seemed to have led every reporter present to believe they are dating, which is exactly what I needed! If the whole world starts thinking they are a couple, then Margaret might also start believing it too. But not everyone seems pleased with the attention the duo has drawn upon themselves. Yara enters the field, looking more serious and aggressive than she usually is and my lips twist into a smirk as I imagine her finding those articles right before her game. Plus, the fact Emma and I are watching the final match from Shi's private box, instead of Yara's, seems to be the cherry on top for my lovely sister-in-law.

***

I have a lot of negative things to say about Yara, but I won't ever deny that she's one hell of an athlete.

I couldn't care less who won the tournament, besides the fact that the winning captain would host the afterparty, but even Shiori and I were on our feet for the final minutes of the championship game, cheering loudly.

Yara, hair streaming behind her like a banner as she stands in the stirrups, leaning low over her horse, led her team to a triumphant victory to the cheers of thousands. Throwing her fists into the air, she accepts the love of her adoring fans. Emma is hypnotized, but who can blame her? Everyone else is riding the wave of her win too.

If Yara had lost, I'd have taken a flight home immediately after the game ended, with or without Emma. But thanks to the media frenzy surrounding Yara, Emma, and Shiori, everyone knows that Yara's sister-in-law is in attendance, and what sort of sister wouldn't come to celebrate her victory?

So here I am, stuck, changing once again in the hotel room into my last piece of evening wear. The silky cornflower blue is a one-piece, cinched at the waist with a flowing bottom half that could easily be mistaken for a skirt. It brings out the sapphire of my eyes, and despite how over the entire weekend I am, I look the part of a supportive socialite sister.

Expensive and put together, but not so flashy that I would outshine Yara.

Just this last event. Just this last event, I keep repeating to myself as I smooth my lipstick over my mouth. It has been a successful trip, even if the split between Yara and Emma hasn't progressed as far as I would have liked, but I'm more than ready to be done. I have homework before my class on Tuesday, and I miss my twins like mad.

I'm surprised when I receive an SMS from Shiori that contains a picture of an invitation she had received for Yara's afterparty, telling me she's going to go even though she knows the invite is just to save face. Yara probably doesn't expect Shiori to show up, considering their spat at the last gathering, but Shi clearly seems to have her own agenda.

We are going to carpool again so Emma and Shi can make an entrance together. In Emma's mind, it's a win-win situation. Showing up with Shiori will ensure that the media never caught wind of her affair with Yara, and at the same time, she can keep up the excuse with Yara that Shiori is simply a coverup. But I know that's not the only reason, even if Emma had fooled herself into thinking otherwise. She wants to spend time with the Japanese artist, and as far as I'm concerned, the more they hang out, the better.

Even more surprising than Shiori's text is the call I receive from Margaret mere minutes before I go to get Emma from her room.

"Hello?" I answer cautiously.

"Well, well, well. It seems you actually pulled it off."

"Hi, Margaret," I say simply.

"The pictures of Emma and her new flame, Shiori, are everywhere, and they look positively smitten with each other. I take it I can rest easy knowing that my daughter's awful affair is finally over?"

Not quite yet, I think, but instead I tell her, "Exactly. It's done. Now there is no animosity between you and me, right?" I don't come right out and mention the sex tape, since Margaret still hasn't admitted to owning a copy, but I'm sure she'll catch my drift.

"Correct. Thank you, Petra. I hope we don't have to speak again for a long while."

"The feeling is mutual," I grumble. "Goodbye, Margaret."

I hang up the phone, feeling both relieved and disingenuous all at once. Emma and Yara are well on the way to being out of each other's lives, but I haven't sealed the deal yet. But what else could I do? I would never admit failure and risk the embarrassment of Margaret releasing that tape.

Hopefully, within the next week or so, my little white lie would become a reality.

***

Okay, I'll also admit that Yara throws one hell of a party too. It seems like somehow she has fit everyone in St. Moritz onto her patio, and everyone seems to practically glow with happiness as they drink, eat, and celebrate the monumental win. Even the losing teams seem to be in good spirits, all the players gathered together in combined pockets laughing.

Shiori and Emma look like the most attractive couple in the world walking into Yara's party together, arm in arm.

Shiori is wearing an emerald-green kimono and Emma has on a beige, form-fitting dress that is covered in black tulle, creating a nude illusion.

Yara has on a clean, pressed version of her team's uniform, and is standing next to the golden St. Moritz Snow Polo World Cup trophy, which is placed on a pedestal. She's posing for pictures, both alone and with her entire team, and fielding questions left and right from the press. It seems her victory was enough to bring everyone's attention back to her.

The party has a distinct air of celebration, but everyone is subdued after the long weekend, especially the other polo players. I suspect under Yara's makeup, she's probably sporting some dark circles too.

I let Emma and Shi go to mingle on their own, having a seat at one of the many tables and observing the area. Just as I suspected, Yara's afterparty is being hosted on her enormous patio overlooking the valley and all the mountains behind it. It's a breathtaking view and the perfect end to three full days of competitions. I didn't play, and even I've had enough.

Yara seems to have noticed Shi and Emma upon their arrival, but she didn't abandon her post near her prize, content for the moment to be the center of attention. Shiori has been drawing gazes from others in the crowd, but the media is remaining solely focused on Yara.

It can't last forever, though. As the night wears on, and drinks flow more freely, Yara makes her way through the party, eventually finding Emma. I'm talking with some of the other guests from New York when I notice the commotion, and I hurry over to intervene.

"I was only congratulating you on your victory," Shiori says, looking unflappable and unbothered.

"Like hell you were," Yara hisses. "You showed up here to feed the rumor mill and get some more news coverage, don't try to tell me otherwise."

"Yara," Emma tries to interject. "Enough."

But Yara doesn't pay any attention to Emma's request and proceeds. "Was it Petra who invited you to St. Moritz?" Yara isn't deterred though, but when Shiori's bodyguard appears, seemingly from thin air, she deflates a bit. Yara seems to realize that she has everyone's attention, but not for the right reasons, and surely she doesn't want to tarnish her very recent victory with a squabble at her own afterparty.

My sister-in-law has everything at the tips of her fingers right now, but she seems to be driven crazy by the one thing she can't control: Emma.

Emma looks torn, but she remains next to Shiori, looking at once embarrassed and tired from the back and forth between her two lovers. Shiori has put up with so much since arriving, and I hate she is once again at the mercy of Yara's sharp tongue.

I reach out to Emma, bringing her close to me, telling her, "We can go back to the hotel right now, if you want. Our flight is at nine in the morning. Maybe it's better we go and get some sleep."

Emma considers the escape plan, and we are both all too aware that Yara and Shiori are waiting for our decision too.

"We don't have to be at this party, and we don't have to be around Yara any longer either," I tell her, my voice just above a whisper.

"Okay," Emma says finally. "I have a lot of thinking to do. I'm ready to leave."

"Emma!" Yara exclaims, trying to keep her voice quiet. "This is not what we discussed."

Emma looks exhausted, shaking her head at Yara. "I'm canceling the plans. Congratulations on the win Yara, but I'm leaving."

Yara sputters, but Shiori takes it all in stride, watching Emma patiently. Emma turns from Yara to Shi, an apologetic note in her voice.

"I'm sorry to you too, Shi."

"I understand. This is not a simple decision for you." Shi's voice is calm and serene. "But I have to ask you something before you leave."

Uh-oh. I remember Shi telling me she wanted to invite Emma to Japan, and I'm sure that's what she's about to do. Even if this is the most inappropriate time possible. I try to say as much, but Shiori continues, cutting me off.

"I have a large exhibition in Tokyo coming up in a few days, and I want you to accompany me, Emma. I'd love to show you my home if you'd allow me." Shi's expression is hopeful but guarded. She knows well that Yara is still standing right there.

Emma, on the other hand, looks devastated. I know that look. It means that she has completely shut down, and there is nothing else that either of these women is going to get from her tonight. I don't want this to become a huge public scene that Emma will regret later, so I have to get her out of here.

"I–" Emma starts. "Shiori, I don't–"

Shi holds a hand up, stopping Emma. "You don't have to answer me right now. You have time to choose. I just wanted you to know, and to allow you all the time you need to think."

Emma nods, exhaling, happy to not have to answer. She's still on the edge though, and Yara is looking more pissed by the second, both by Emma paying her no mind and Shiori's invitation. I really need to get her out of this party and away from Yara's house before she regrets it.

"Let's go," I coax, simultaneously texting the driver to be waiting for us outside.

Emma looks at Yara one more time before letting me lead her out.

"This isn't over," Yara snaps before turning her back on us and disappearing among the crowd. I'm not sure if Emma will have it in her to follow me instead of Yara, so I hustle her to the car as fast as I can. Fortunately, neither Yara nor Shiori retain us and we make our way outside and to the car.

We get in the back seat just as fast, and as soon as we're behind closed doors, Emma finally relaxes, and the curses start flowing.

"What the fuck is wrong with me!" she yells, punching the seat in front of her. "How could I just fucking… shut down in front of everyone like a coward." She clutches her head in her hands, leaning over. "I almost outed Yara and me. I was so close to yelling at her. Shit. Fuck."

"Hey, hey," I rub small circles on her back, letting her rant. "It's fine. We're out of there. It's over."

"Did Shiori really just invite me to Japan?" Emma asks, her voice small once she's calmed down a few notches.

"She did," I confirm. "How does that make you feel?"

"Happy. Confused. And pissed off."

"Why pissed off?"

"Because." Emma leans back in her seat and closes her eyes. "I'm sure you've gathered that I've caught feelings for Yara, and despite her being a bitch all weekend, they're still there. When she won that game, I wanted to kiss her on her stupid mouth so badly, and Shiori was sitting right there next to me." She looks at me with pleading eyes. "Petra, what do I do? Should I go?"

I take the time to consider it. I know Emma's feelings for Yara are still present, and raw, and they haven't even called things off permanently yet. On the other hand, Emma loves to travel, and some time far away from Yara would give her the clarity to think.

"Go to Japan," I say firmly. "Don't stay at Shiori's place but go. Let her take you around, show you her exhibit. But explore on your own too." I nod, pretty confident at my advice. "Go to Japan, Em. You need to get away, even if it's just for a little while."

Emma releases a shuddering breath, and laughs shakily, nodding. "You're right. I know you're right. I have never been to Tokyo before anyway. It's gonna be dope for sure."

"I agree, it's gonna be amazing." I give her a one arm embrace, squeezing her tight against me. "And it's gonna be great for you to ponder your relationship with Yara."

"Thanks, babe."

She hugs me back, and I feel like I can finally see the light at the end of the tunnel with getting Yara away from my best friend, who I love so dearly. "You're so welcome, Emma."

CHAPTER 11

St. Moritz, January 31, 2022
Petra

While I slept pretty well through the night, especially knowing today I'm gonna fly back to Manhattan, the same can't be said of Emma as I make my way inside her room in the early morning.

Even though we waited to have breakfast on the plane, to catch a few more minutes of sleep, Emma looks tired and a bundle of nerves. One of the hotel's butlers finishes getting her luggage ready, while Emma is sipping an espresso made from her coffee machine. I notice she isn't wearing any makeup, and the big dark circles under her eyes give me the impression she didn't sleep much with everything that happened last night.

I walk in her direction, and once I stand beside her, I lean in and greet her with a kiss on the head. "Did you get some sleep at least?" I ask in a low voice.

She shakes her head as she finishes her espresso, her face emotionless and unreadable. Then heaving a long sigh, she says, "Not at all."

"I know it's a hard decision," I comment, knowing flying back with me today wasn't in her plans at all. "But you are doing the right thing."

"I know, Yara really crossed the line yesterday."

My heart squeezes tight as I watch Emma trying her best to keep her composure as she processes all the disrespect Yara infringed on her and Shi. I rub her back to give her some strength, knowing how hard this moment must be—the moment she finally realizes how nasty she'd been letting someone treat her and her beloved ones. The fact Yara treated Shi like crap in front of everyone without any bother seems to have been the last straw for Emma.

"I'm very proud of you," I tell her from the bottom of my heart. Before it gets too awkward, I ask the butler to take our luggage down while I go and give a last check around our rooms to make sure we don't leave anything behind.

Once Emma is ready, we finish checking out and leave the Badrutt's Palace Hotel one last time. Before we get into the car though, I ask the doorman to take a picture of my best friend and me standing in front of the hotel's beautiful entrance and wooden revolving doors. After he snatches a few pictures, I show them to Emma, managing to pull from her a trace of a smile. At the very least, we will have a few memories from our weekend in St. Moritz.

The drive to the airport is disturbingly quiet as Emma remains looking out of the window, totally engrossed in her thoughts.

Her big black sunglasses hide nearly half of her face, and I imagine she put them on in order to hide the pain she's going through in silence. When our plane finally gets into view, I lay my hand on hers, reminding her I'm here. "Once we take off, you'll feel much better."

She sniffles in reply, never turning away from the window.

"What the fuck?" Emma spits out as she points a finger at the glass, her face turning to me to catch my attention.

I follow her gaze and look out of the window, only to be smashed with the worst kind of view possible.

"Holy shit," I snap, unable to say anything else.

"What is Yara doing here?" Emma asks me, totally taken aback that the staff let her go to the tarmac and stand in front of our plane. I imagine they thought she wanted to tell us goodbye, but she's the last person we wanted to see here!

The car park is not too far away from the plane, and I feel anxious. *Damn, I can't believe that snake is here.* My heartbeat is already bouncing hard inside my chest as I watch Emma take longer than usual to leave the car.

"I'm here, alright?" I say, giving her a little squeeze on the hand. "Just go first, and don't stop until you are inside the plane."

She nods at me while taking a deep breath in. After mentally getting herself ready, Emma leaves the car and I follow suit.

I walk towards the staircase with my heart in my throat, while Yara's gaze is pinned on Emma, who is closer to her.

"Are you really leaving?" Yara snaps, her arms folded over her chest.

"I am, yeah," Emma answers, her big black frames hiding the dark circles under her eyes from the heartache. "The tournament is over."

"I'm gonna stay a few more days," Yara announces, her tone deeply serious. "I thought you might do the same."

Seeing how Yara is trying to dissuade Emma, I step in and take over. "She already said she's leaving, Yara."

"You better stay out of this, snake!" Yara snarls, her gaze nearly shooting daggers at me, and it really does feel like a threat. Her gaze returns to Emma, and her features deepen. "So? Are you really gonna leave me here alone in St. Moritz, Emma?"

"Yara, the plane is waiting," I interpose. I put my hand on Emma's back, pushing her slightly to get to the stairs. "Em, let's go."

"Let Emma speak for God's sake!"

I know exactly what Yara is trying to do: if she persuades Emma to stay, her influence will win her over, and Emma will never go to Tokyo afterward.

"I am," Emma manages to spit out. I shut my eyes tight, barely believing what Emma just said. I know how damn hard this must be for her. "I have to go. Goodbye, Yara."

But Yara reaches out and grabs Emma's arm right away, halting her in her tracks. Emma becomes immediately confused at Yara's aggression, but before she can even say a word, Yara takes over. "I'm gonna be very clear with you: if you go to Tokyo with Shi, we are done."

I remain silent, totally taken aback by her statement, but at the end of the day, I knew an ultimatum would happen. It was inevitable.

"Get your hand off of me!" Emma pulls her arm away with enough strength that Yara releases her, and without further ado, she keeps walking up the stairs until she finally gets inside the plane.

I do the same, ignoring my sister-in-law as much as I can, but as soon as I step a foot on the staircase, Yara bars the way, extending her arm in front of me. My first reaction is to call security to step in, but before I can even open my mouth, she leans towards me and says, "One day or another, you're gonna regret what you did. It might take time, but you will regret it."

Here we are, one more threat from my lovely sister-in-law. "Are you done?" I ask, never letting my guard down.

Yara finally drops her arm and without saying anything further, marches back to her car, taking her annoyance with her.

I let out a sigh of relief as I watch her get inside her black sedan.

"Is everything alright, Miss?" one of the airport staff asks.

"Yes," I answer, putting on a smile as I finish climbing the stairs.

I never thought Yara would continue to threaten me without scruples, but right now all I want is to go and check how my best friend is doing.

Reaching inside, my gaze lands on Emma who's already on her seat, sipping some alcoholic drink, her big sunglasses still on.

It hurts to see her like this, but words can't describe how proud I am of her to have stood up against Yara.

All I can hope is that Yara will finally leave her alone.

TO BE CONTINUED...